A RABBIT'S TALE
An Easter Story

Diogenes Ruiz

ISBN:097631262X
ISBN-13: 978-0976312628

This book is dedicated to my wonderful wife, Karin.

TABLE OF CONTENTS

1 THE NEW NEIGHBORS 7

2 SPECIAL DELIVERY 19

3 THE PRAYING MANTIS 25

4 TWENTY FIVE YEARS LATER...31

5 THE DEVIL'S APPRENTICE 37

6 FATHER'S KEEPER? 41

7 JUAN'S RECRUITMENT 51

8 BD109 55

9 GOOD NEWS BAD NEWS 61

10 LEIGH 67

11 DUTY CALLS 75

12 THE EASTER BUNNY ARRIVES 81

13 DIAGNOSIS: RABBIT 85

14 POST-TRAUMATIC RABBIT SYNDROME 95

15 THE DISCRIMINATED RABBIT...99

16 RAY MEETS THE DEVIL...105

17 RABBITS NEED NOT APPLY 111

18 HAVING A BAD DAY?...117

19 NECESSARY ALLIANCE 123

20 SCOUT'S HONOR 127

21 RABBIT'S GOTTA WORK 133

22 THE EMPEROR'S NEW CLOTHES 137

23 RABBITS WELCOME...145

24 MANIC MONDAY 153

25 THE NEW IMPROVED MONTY 161

26 MISSION IMPOSSIBLE...165

27 THE LITTLE RED HOUSE 181

28 THE REUNION 187

29 LOOKING FOR ANSWERS.. 191

30 TWO YEARS LATER 195

EPILOGUE 197

****

CONNECTING MORE OF THE DOTS 199

QUESTIONS TO CONSIDER 200

FOR THOSE OF YOU THAT ARE SEARCHING............................... 201

ACKNOWLEDGEMENTS... 203

ABOUT THE AUTHOR 205

TO MY READERS 206

1

The New Neighbors

It was Wednesday, the week after Thanksgiving. Juan caught the aroma of his mom's cooking, spaghetti and meatballs, his favorite. His stomach grumbled as he finished his homework and headed downstairs to check the mail, again. The mailbox was still empty. He checked the usual spot where his parents put the mail until they had time to sort through it. Yesterday's pile had not changed. "Mom, how come we didn't get any mail today?"

Maria continued preparing dinner as she glanced at Juan. "It's by the computer."

"No it's not. This is yesterday's mail."

She thought for a moment. "I got the mail earlier, on my way to the market. I think I might have left it in the car. Can you check for me?

Juan ran out and opened Maria's car door. There it was, on the passenger seat. He grabbed the pile of mail and sifted through it, more junk and some of the usual envelopes. One seemed to contain a plastic card inside. He looked back in the car to make sure he did not miss a piece of mail. *"It's not here, bummer."*

"I got the mail. It was in the car."

"Thanks, dear. Are you waiting for something to come in the mail?"

"Yeah, I ordered ..."

The front door opened and his dad walked in. "Man, it smells good in here."

"Hi Ron, you're just in time. We're just about ready to eat."

"Great, cause I'm starved."

"Juan, can you get your sister, while I finish preparing dinner? It's time to eat." Maria was a preschool teacher, and her husband Ron was a programmer for a large software company in Cary, North Carolina. They were good parents and the bedroom community of Cary suited them fine. Maria's work schedule gave her the flexibility to prepare dinner for her family.

Ron and Maria were practical people. Although they had both been raised Catholic, they were not practicing Catholics. They attended their local church on Christmas and Easter, as a nostalgic ritual from their youth. That was about as far as they wanted their religious influence to go.

Early on in their marriage, Ron and Maria agreed on two priorities. The first was to eat dinner together as a family as often as possible. Second, was their decision not to burden their two kids with religious baggage.

Angie was the youngest and had recently started second grade. Juan was her big brother, a fifth grader.

Juan was not an athletic kid. He preferred to read and take pictures, lots of them. There was something magical about taking a picture. He could see something everybody else could see, and yet, it was his way of looking at it that made it unique. He would see texture and the juxtaposition of elements, where most people saw a bunch of rocks, or he would see the interplay of light and shadow as they created exquisite patterns, where most people saw a rusty toolbox.

Ron Arias sat dizzy with anticipation of Maria's spaghetti. Juan and Angie sat down. Maria put out the garlic bread and took her seat, then came a knock at the door. They were not expecting company. Ron made a face and used all of his will power to tear himself away from his freshly served plate of spaghetti and meatballs. When he answered the door, he was greeted by a tall gentleman in his forties. His well sculpted chin and thin mustache reminded Ron of Errol Flynn, one of his favorite movie stars from the 1930's. Alongside the stranger, there stood a boy. He appeared to be the man's son. At once, Errol Flynn smiled and held out his hand to shake Ron's hand.

"Good evening, I'm Blake McPride, and this is my son

Monty. We've rented the house across the street for a couple of months until the one we are building is completed. This was in our mailbox, but I believe it belongs to you. The mail carrier placed it in our box by mistake."

Ron took the magazine. He figured that it was probably delivered as a promotional trial since he had not ordered it. He did not invite them in. His stomach was grumbling, and all he could think about was his spaghetti and meatballs getting cold. He wanted to keep this short and not appear to be rude, but the spaghetti was calling. "Why, thank you." He held out his hand. "It's good to meet you both. Welcome to the neighborhood. If there is anything we can do to help you get situated, just let us know."

"Thank you, Ron. Well, goodnight. Come on, Monty."

Just then, Maria came up behind Ron, "Who's at the door?"

"This is Mr. Blake McPride and his son Monty. They are renting the house across the street for a couple of months until the construction of their new home is completed. This is my wife, Maria."

"It's nice to meet you Mr. McPride, and you too Monty."

By now Juan and Angie were also at the door. Maria put her hands on their shoulders. "This is our son Juan and our daughter Angie."

Mr. McPride smiled at each of the children. "It's nice to meet you both."

Monty kept silent and looked off to the side. He did not seem interested in this ritualistic formal introduction.

Maria raised her hand and motioned to them. "Won't you come in, we're just about to sit down and have dinner? There is plenty. Where is Mrs. McPride? She is welcome to join us as well."

"My wife passed away a few years ago. It's just the two of us now." Mr. McPride glanced at Monty and then back at Maria. "Thank you for your generous invitation. Monty and I have reservations at Chateau Croix. I'm having dinner with a colleague. There's some last-minute company business that needs attention before the big move."

"Oh, I see." Maria felt bad that the boy had lost his mother. She wondered how, but did not want to pry. "I'm so sorry about

Mrs. McPride."

Blake McPride paused for a moment. "Thank you, yes, we miss her very much." Monty remained silent and continued to look off into space.

Maria wondered what the new neighbor did for a living. "What kind of business are you in, Mr. McPride?"

Ron froze at the thought of having to stand at the door much longer while their dinner got cold. Why on earth did his wife want to prolong this conversation? Surely this was not the time to get into a question and answer session with the new neighbors. His stomach growled and he pictured his fresh hot spaghetti turning into a clump of petrified mess. He would need a chisel and hammer instead of a knife and fork.

"We develop products for the medical industry. The company is being relocated to Research Triangle Park from Sacramento." He looked at his watch. "Well, we'd better get going. I don't want to be late for my dinner meeting. Thank you again for your hospitable invitation."

Ron and Maria waved. Maria said goodbye for the Arias family. "It was nice to meet you. Let us know if you need anything."

Blake McPride waved as he and Monty turned to leave.

Ron quickly closed the door and made a beeline back to the dinner table. Maria and Angie followed.

Juan remained and peeked through the curtain as the new neighbors left. *"The new boy must be a couple of years older,"* Juan thought. *"Maybe he's from another planet."* There was something about him that made Juan uneasy. Maybe it was the way he looked into space while his father was talking. He thought about it for a moment, but that wasn't it. It was the way Monty glanced at him occasionally with what seemed to be a glare of anger. Maybe it was nothing, Juan thought. *"Maybe I just imagined him giving me a dirty look."* Then, as he was about to head back to the dinner table, he saw Monty fall behind just enough to be out of Mr. McPride's view. Monty looked around quickly to make sure nobody was watching. Juan crouched down behind the curtain. *"What was this new kid up to?"*

As Juan continued his surveillance, Monty turned and quietly deposited a ferociously large glob of spit on the Arias mail box handle. Nobody suspected that he was accumulating his mega spit bomb as his father spoke with Maria and Ron. At last, he released it on its target. It oozed down the sides of the handle and the front of the mailbox. Monty looked at it and was glad of the slimy surprise which he hoped would be evident to the next person who opened the mailbox. He shuffled to catch up to his father, but before he did, he quickly glanced at the small crack in the sheer curtains and spotted Juan looking at him. Juan's heart thumped. He was sure it would pop out of his chest. He froze with horror as he realized that he had been spotted. Monty's look clearly conveyed, "If you tell, you're dead." The look was punctuated with a creepy smile. Then Monty turned and caught up to his father, already halfway across the street. Juan made a dash for the dining room table and sat down looking at his plate of spaghetti.

Ron took a bite of his food. "It looks like we have new neighbors, at least temporarily. Hmm honey, you make the best spaghetti. I couldn't wait to get rid of them so we could get down to business and eat."

"Ron, I know you were eager to get rid of them, but we have to be polite. They seem nice enough, too bad about his wife passing away. The son looks to be about Juan's age, maybe a little older. What did you think of Monty, Juan? Perhaps you can be friends and help him make the transition to his new home?" Maria observed that Juan was not eating. "What's the matter, honey? You haven't touched your food."

"I'm not hungry, lost my appetite."

Maria touched Juan's forehead to feel for fever. "Are you feeling OK? Spaghetti and meatballs are your favorite."

"I feel fine." His thoughts were on what he had just witnessed as he wondered what to do. This new kid looked a little crazy. Perhaps it best not to tell and just hose down the mailbox after dinner. "No, I'm fine, mom, just not hungry."

Ron held up the magazine. "Oh, and they delivered this."

Juan looked up at Ron. Then he recognized the item his father was holding. He popped out of his seat, ran over and snatched the magazine out of Ron's hands. He ran back, sat down, and placed it neatly on the table.

"Hey, pal, what's going on? You grabbed that as though your life depended on it."

"It does!" He flipped through the pages. "I ordered a subscription."

Maria and Ron looked at each other and then back to their son. "You did? Why?"

"Cause it has the best photography ever. That's why. I saved my allowance and used it to get a three-year subscription."

"Three years? You might not even like the magazine in three years."

Juan ignored his Dad's comment and started to shove spaghetti into his mouth as he carefully turned the pages. He didn't want to get any sauce on them.

Maria noticed how her son was eating. He reminded her of a hungry caveman. "Got your appetite back, huh? Speaking of photography, what were you taking pictures of out in the back yard this afternoon?"

Juan took a break from gazing at his magazine. "We have to take photos for a project in school."

"What kind of project?" asked Ron.

"We have to take pictures of Easter stuff. You know, rabbits, eggs, stuff like that."

Ron was a little annoyed that his son should be involved in this kind of project. After all, they were in a public school, and religion has no place in school. "Why is Mrs. Arnold having you do that kind of project? She's is not supposed to be teaching religion, is she?"

"No, we don't have religion class, Dad. We're learning about different people and their customs and rituals. The next one is going to be on Chanukah. She wants us to learn about them, that's all."

Ron looked at Maria. She knew how strongly he felt about keeping religion out of school. There was no place for "God" or other superstitions in today's fast-paced world. Those who believed in such nonsense were usually the uneducated or people who had some kind of guilt or insecurity that could probably be cured by a few sessions of good psychotherapy, not a life of religion and idol worship. Ron was proud to be head of his secular family.

Maria ignored Ron's frustration. "I'm sure you'll do well, dear. Now close your magazine and finish your dinner. You can look at it afterwards."

Ron chimed in. "What a waste of time. If you asked me, they should be learning about computer programming. It's the future!"

"I hate computer programming." Juan knew where this conversation was heading. He could mouth the words. His father said the same thing every time.

"Better that than a starving artist, Juan."

"I'd rather be starving photographer than a computer nerd!"

Maria looked at Ron. He knew what she was thinking. *"Do you have to start with that again?"* She turned to Juan. "Now, now, let's not argue. You'll have plenty of time to figure out what you want to do."

Juan was undeterred. "I know what I want to do. I want to take pictures for this, *National Geographic*, the best magazine in the world!" He was defiant as he held up his prized copy. His subscription was official. It was like a rite of passage. Photography was his life.

Ron stared at the familiar yellow border of the magazine in Juan's hand. His brief sense of nostalgia was overtaken by his sense of practicality. "Printed magazines are going to be a thing of the past very soon."

Juan's excitement was not at all deflated by his father's comment. "That's all right, they still need good pictures."

Angie, chimed in to support her big brother. "Yeah, they still need good 'pittures.'"

"I'm writing a letter to National Geographic so I can work for them one day."

After dinner, Juan took out the hose, connected it to the spigot and hosed down the mailbox while his parents were watching television. Nobody saw him, he thought.

The next morning, Juan and Angie headed off to PS189. Angie liked having her big brother at the same school. He always looked after her.

Today, Ms. Arnold gave the class a series of equations involving fractions. Juan was good at math. Although they were being timed, he had no trouble with most of them. A few were tricky, but he wasn't fooled at all.

Just as the clock struck 10:00, Ms. Arnold asked the class

to put down their pencils. After collecting the papers, she stepped outside for a few minutes.

As Ms. Arnold entered the classroom, Juan's heart sank. He was stricken with disbelief and fear as his teacher escorted Monty into the classroom.

"Class, may I have your attention please," she said with a big welcoming smile. "I would like to introduce you to the newest member of our class, Monty McPride. I know you will all help me make Monty feel right at home." Then she looked at Monty. "Welcome Monty. Here, let me show you to your seat."

Juan was certain that this was a bad omen. The weird new neighbor was now in his class. *"This is so unfair. Why couldn't he move to the desert or someplace far away?"* Juan pretended to look at his book, but he could feel Monty's gaze upon him. At least there was no way Monty could sit next to him. There was only one empty desk, and it was two rows over. That was a relief.

Then Ms. Arnold asked Becky Pearson to move to the vacant desk. Monty would need to use the larger desk; he was a big boy. Juan was horrified at the realization that the easygoing classmate with the ponytails that sat next to him was being replaced with his neighbor from hell.

"What are the odds of this happening?" Juan thought. *"I must be the unluckiest kid on the planet. My life is over. Not only do I have to live close to this spit-bomb puking lunatic, but now he will be lurking at my side in school, casting whatever poison he has my way. Maybe I should pretend to faint or pass out. That would get me out of here now, but I would be right back in this seat tomorrow. There is no escaping. What are the mathematical odds? Is there a scientific explanation for this? There must be. My dad says that everything can be explained by scientific reasoning if we take time and examine the facts. What are the facts? Rich crazy kid moves in across the street. Rich crazy kid spits all over my mailbox. Rich crazy kid is assigned to my class and winds up sitting right next to me."* Juan closed his eyes, dreading the inevitable.

"Hey loser," came the soft whisper in his ear. Juan didn't bother to look at Monty. He pretended to be listening to Ms. Arnold. Juan sighed. He looked down onto his pad in an attempt to avoid Monty. All at once, Juan let out a yell and jumped up from his desk. He backed up and tripped over the person sitting on the other side. There was a crash. The class froze. All eyes were upon him. He was breathing hard as he struggled to get up and shoo away the large centipede that was on his note pad. It was a big black juicy one.

Juan pointed at the centipede, and the class issued a collective "eeeeeww."

"Where did that come from?" asked Ms. Arnold.

"I don't know." Juan looked at Monty suspiciously.

Ms. Arnold was disgusted. She did not want to have to pick the thing up.

"Here, Ms. Arnold, I can help," Monty proudly announced, as he leaned over and picked up the large squirming insect. "What should I do with it?"

Ms. Arnold made a hurried gesture with her hands. "Just get rid of it. Open the window and let it out onto the grass."

"Yes, ma'am," Monty said politely as he went to the window. He leaned out, holding the centipede in his palm. "There, little fella," he said in a gentle, caring voice. Then he tightened his fist until the centipede exploded in his hand. "That's better." Monty wiped his hand on the outside brick to get rid of most of the insect debris before leaning back in. "OK, he's safe now."

"Thank you, Monty. Now, take your seat, you too, Juan. Let's get on with class, shall we?"

"Yes, ma'am," responded Monty in his noblest, best behavior voice.

Juan looked at Monty in disbelief. Monty gave him the same sick smile that Juan had seen the night before.

"OK, everyone, remember that your pictures for our culture and rituals class are due next week. I hope you're giving some thought to your photographs. There will be first, second and third place winners who will receive homework passes. We will review the photos as we learn about what this day represents for Catholics. Next, we will explore the Chanukah celebration among the Jewish people. Are there any Catholics in this class who can share a little about Easter?"

Approximately a third of the class raised their hands. Juan was not sure whether he should raise his. He knew that his parents were raised Catholic, but he didn't know what he was, or what being Catholic entailed. They did not go to church much, and he never asked about it. Juan remembered the last two times they attended Mass, on Christmas and Easter. There was singing and people read stuff to the audience. Today was definite proof that there was no such thing as God. He would never have allowed Monty to move in next door and sit next to him at school, but he would research Easter a bit. He was sure he could do well with his photo entry.

Ms. Arnold looked around at the kids with their hands raised. "Freddie, tell the class what Easter represents."

Freddie lowered his hand. "It's when we get to buy new clothes and stuff we want. Not like Christmas when other people give you presents. This is mostly stuff you eat or wear, like chocolate covered bunnies, or a new shirt or pair of pants."

"OK, very good, Freddie." Several other hands went up. "Yes, Adrienne, go ahead."

"I think it has something to do with Jesus, the man they killed on the cross. He was supposed to come back to life or something like that."

"OK, one more. Yes, Henry."

Henry stood up. "At first, everyone liked him, then nobody liked him. Then after they killed him, some people thought he was the son of God because he came back to life." Henry seemed very proud of his knowledge.

"OK, very good, Henry. Now class, whether you believe in God or not is not the point. We are exploring beliefs of different cultures and groups of people so that we can better understand them and get along. All right, let's move on to our English grammar lesson."

At lunch, Juan sat with some of his classmates.

Monty strolled over to his table and shoved to make room for himself. He sat down between Juan and Henry. "I know you saw me last night, loser." He whispered to Juan. "That was my little gift to you and your family. I was extremely disappointed that you washed it off. You should be more appreciative."

Juan was repulsed as he thought of Monty's grotesque antics. "You're sick."

"And you're dead if you tell anyone. Just like I squished that stupid centipede, I'll squish you and wipe your guts on your sister's dress."

Juan wondered how someone could be so nasty. "Why do you do it?"

Monty turned to him and whispered, "Because I hate you, your family, this stupid school and everyone in it. I hate everything."

"Why do you hate everything and why do you hate me? I've never done anything to you."

Monty turned to Juan and opened his mouth wide, to expose the partially chewed food. Juan cringed with disgust. Monty smiled his sick grin seeing Juan's reaction. "That's why. Because it's fun. Because I can. You should try it. Then you wouldn't be such a loser."

"No thanks!" Juan got up and started to take his tray to another table. Monty stuck out his leg and tripped him. Juan started to fall. Henry leaned out and prevented him from going all the way down and spilling his lunch.

Monty looked honestly disappointed and made a pouty face. Then he turned to Henry. "Hey, stupido, what do you think you're doing?" He then opened his mouth to expose his partially chewed food for Henry to see.

2

Special Delivery

When Juan got home that afternoon, Maria called for him. "Juan, honey, I need you to do me a favor. Get the hose and wash down the mailbox, inside and out." Juan looked at his mother with surprise. Last night's mailbox wash and the spit bomb removal had been quite thorough. Did he miss a spot?

"Why mom, what's with the mailbox?" Juan knew that she was upset because she spoke in an excessively calm voice.

"Honey, the mail carrier left our mail next door with the Jansens because some crazy person left the remains of a dead squirrel in our mailbox. The poor old man almost had a heart attack when he opened it and saw it in there. I need you to get a stick or something and put it in a garbage bag. Then I need you to hose the mailbox down to get rid of the blood and remaining gunk that is smeared inside. I called it in and filed a vandalism report. The police said that we need to do the cleaning up ourselves. I can't imagine what sick sort of person would do such a thing."

Juan was stunned. He had seen lots of scary movies with vampires and monsters, but Monty was scarier because he was real and creepy in an evil sort of way.

Later that night, as the family sat down to eat dinner, Juan asked, "Mom, do you believe in God?"

Maria glanced at Ron then back at Juan. "Why sure, dear."

Ron rolled his eyes and added, "Some people like to believe in a God. It makes them feel better."

"You mean like Santa Claus?" Juan asked.

"I guess it's something like that. It makes them feel better about things."

Juan persisted. "Yeah, but is there really a God? I mean people go to church and pray and all that kind of stuff, and we go at Christmas and Easter. Is there a God for them?"

Ron rolled his eyes again. "It's just a belief, son. It doesn't need to be real. Folks just take comfort in pretending a God is there."

Maria looked at Ron. "Well, I don't share your father's view completely. I believe there is a real God who is there for everyone. People have their own way of believing or not believing that He is there. When you are older you can decide for yourself if there is or isn't a God, and what that means for you. Your father and I don't want to pressure you into believing in something that you otherwise might not accept. Why do you ask?"

Juan explained his class assignment. "Ms. Arnold was talking about different cultures and beliefs and asked if there were any Catholics in the class who could explain what Easter was about. I didn't know if I was Catholic or not. You were both brought up Catholic, but I wasn't sure what that made me. Is someone Catholic just because their parents are Catholic?"

Maria gave Juan an endearing look. "You can be Catholic until you decide what you want to be, if anything. When you're older, you can make up your own mind, OK?"

Juan paused and looked first at his father, then at his mother. "Is it all right if I believe there is a God?"

Maria smiled. "Of course, honey. Now eat your food."

Ron looked at Maria with a frown but did not say a word. The family ate quietly for a few minutes and then Juan started with questions again. "Mom, what *did* happen on Easter?"

Ron got up and left the table, taking his dinner plate with him. "Come on, Angie, eat with daddy in the living room." Angie just shook her head to say, no.

"OK, suit yourself." He went into the living room by himself.

Maria turned her attention to Juan. "What little I know about Easter is that Jesus was crucified. They nailed him to a cross on a Friday. He died, and three days later, he rose from the dead and went to heaven. On Easter Sunday, that's what we celebrate."

"Why was he killed? Did he kill somebody or do something terrible?"

"No. That's a little more complicated. Jesus was the son of God. He helped many people, taught them things and cured many of them. He even brought back one of his dear friends from death. His name was Lazarus."

"Why couldn't Jesus save himself from being killed if he could bring the other man back from the dead? Why didn't God save his son from being killed, if he was God? Couldn't he do that?"

Maria was starting to feel a little uneasy. She didn't know how to answer her son's questions, which were growing in complexity. Finally, she said, "Well, honey, I'm not quite sure, but there was probably a good reason."

"Does God have a wife?"

Maria sighed. "That's enough for tonight, Juan. Eat your dinner, dear."

Angie sat quietly and then broke the silence with a loud fart. Maria and Juan looked up and started to laugh. Angie giggled after seeing their reaction.

The next few days at school were excruciating for Juan. No more dead things appeared in the mailbox, but sitting next to Monty, there was constant bullying, nose picking, bug squashing, and gross displays of the contents of Monty's mouth. Many of the kids in the class tried to avoid their hellish classmate. Even Ms. Arnold seemed to be growing tired of Monty's tricks and his pretense of being an angel. He was sent to the principal's office more in one week than anybody else had gone all year long.

It was the night before Juan's photo was due for the class project about Easter. During dinner, Ron asked, "How is the new boy doing, Juan? I understand that he's in your class."

Juan responded without hesitation. "He's a jerk!"

Angie repeated, "Yeah, he's a jerk!"

Ron and Maria both looked at each other with surprise.

"That's not nice," Maria said. "Why are you calling him that? He and his dad seemed nice when they came to the door."

Ron glanced at Maria. "The father's loaded! You know that company that is being relocated? He owns it. I checked it out.

McPride Industries is huge. They have contracts with every major hospital. The guy must be worth millions, easy."

Juan shrugged his shoulders. "Yeah, he may be rich, but he's still a jerk and a bully. He's mean and nasty and pushes everyone around."

Maria could not believe that Monty was as bad as all that. "I'm sure he'll adjust. After all, it can be difficult moving to a new place."

Juan was astonished that his mother could be so naive. "I wished they had moved somewhere else."

"You should try to be his friend. Maybe he's lonely and has difficulty making friends."

Ron glanced over to Maria then at Juan. "I'm sure it'll be all right. Just don't let him bully you around."

Juan looked at his dad. *"How can a grown-up be so stupid? That kid is twice my size, and he's probably repeated fifth grade fifty times."*

Ron continued, "Who knows, you two might become best buddies!"

Juan almost barfed at the thought, but kept silent, finished his dinner and went to his room.

At school the next morning, just before they were about to go in, Angie seemed troubled and was nearly in tears.

"What's the matter, Angie?"

She looked up at him with disappointment in her face. "I forgot my lunch."

Big brother Juan came to her rescue as he always did when something was troubling her. "Here, take mine. I'm going to be busy at lunch anyway and won't have time to eat. You might as well take it."

Angie's little face beamed. "Thank you, Juan."

"No problem. You better go in."

No sooner had Juan taken out his lunch to give it to Angie than Monty walked by and knocked the lunch bag out of his hands.

"Whoops! Sorry, losers."

Juan picked up the lunch bag and gave it to Angie. "Don't mind him. He's an idiot." He reassured her. Juan continued to his locker and then stopped into the boy's bathroom. Monty followed him in. Juan was not aware that he had been ambushed.

"So you think I'm an idiot?" Monty raged as he pushed Juan.

"No, I think you're a jerk!" Juan surprised himself standing up to this crazy loon.

Monty had a crazed look in his eyes. He pushed Juan hard enough to knock him to the ground. The book and papers in his hands went flying. They fell onto the white tile floor. Monty looked like a madman. He wanted to hurt Juan badly. Then out of the corner of his eye he caught sight of Juan's photo. He also spotted a letter of some kind and picked it up.

"What's this?" Monty read the letter out loud. "Dear National Geographic, my name is Juan Arias and I really like your magazine. I am a recent subscriber and enjoy your fine photographs. When I'm older I would like to apply for…"

Monty looked at Juan, then back at the letter and started to laugh hysterically. "You dweeb, you're such a nerd!" He crumpled the letter and threw it on the floor. Then he spotted the photo. "What do we have here?"

Juan got up and tried to grab it out of Monty's hands. "It's my entry for the photography contest. Give it back."

Monty shoved Juan back again. "Hmm, you know, I was going to enter, but I just didn't get around to taking a picture. So, loser, I guess I'll be in it after all. This will have to do."

Juan stood up and tried to grab his picture back. "You can't do that. That's my picture!"

Monty shoved Juan hard to the floor again. "Listen, dufus, I can do whatever I want and you better keep your mouth shut or some nasty things are going to happen to you."

Juan got back up in a hurry as he continued to try to get his picture back. "I don't care, give it back!" Monty gave another hard shove, but this time Juan did not fall to the floor.

"Oh, did I say you, loser? I meant your loser sister. You say one word about this and your cute little sister is not going to be so cute anymore." As he said this, he pulled out a rather large knife and pinned it under Juan's throat. "She'll look more like that squirrel I left for you. You remember it, don't you, the mailbox surprise?" He gazed at Juan, enjoying the moment, taking it all in and feeling wonderful about his power. Then he gave Juan a full creepy smile. "And I mean it, loser!" Monty then looked at himself in the mirror, threw himself a kiss and left the bathroom.

Juan picked up his books and the rest of his papers, including the crumpled letter, and cleaned himself up. His neck was a little sore where Monty had poked him with the knife. As Juan examined the area on his neck, he saw a few drops of blood where the knife had made contact with his skin. "God help me," Juan said as he looked in the mirror. "And please don't let anything bad happen to Angie."

3

The Praying Mantis

Juan sat in his chair gazing at his notebook, lost in thought, when Ms. Arnold announced, "OK, class make sure you put your photographs on my desk this morning before we get started. I'll take a look at them during lunch and announce the winners of the free homework passes this afternoon, before we begin our lesson on culture and rituals." The kids lined up. One by one they placed their photos on Ms. Arnold's desk.

As Monty got up from his desk, he whispered to Juan, "Remember what I told you, snot maggot, or your little sister is dead meat."

Juan remained in his seat as Monty got in line to hand in the stolen picture. When it was his turn, he politely smiled at Ms. Arnold and put the picture on her desk. Then he beamed a big friendly smile to her.

"Thank you, Monty," Ms. Arnold replied.

As the line continued to move, Ms. Arnold noticed that Juan had not gotten in line. "Juan, don't you have an entry for the class assignment?"

From his desk, Juan looked up and uttered in a low voice, "No, ma'am."

"And why not? I've seen you take plenty of pictures; you love photography."

Juan tried to find the right response. He fumbled his words. "Uh um, I lost it and didn't have time to take another one."

Ms. Arnold looked disappointed and a little irritated. "You realize that this is part of your homework assignment, and I will have to give you a failing grade on it."

Juan wondered what Ms. Arnold would think if she knew all Monty had done and that he was a diabolical bully. It was amazing that she had not caught on to him by now. *"Why are grownups so blind to things?"* He wondered, but he dared not say a word. He remembered the dead squirrel in his mailbox and the threats Monty had made to hurt Angie.

"Yes, ma'am" Juan acknowledged as he sat slumped in his chair looking down at his blank notebook. He felt Monty's creepy gaze upon him. It was followed by a whisper.

"That's a good little snot maggot."

Juan did his best to ignore the demon child next to him. *"God, I don't know if you are real or not, but if you are real, please help me."*

The morning dragged on and then it was finally time for lunch. Juan, Henry, Adrianne, and a few other kids were gathered in the playground. They formed a circle and were hunched over, looking at something on the ground.

Monty came out and yelled at the group, "Any of you phlegm maggots wanna jump the fence and get a shake across the street?"

"You know, you're not supposed to do that," cried Henry.

Monty approached the group. "Hey, Henrico stupido, I do whatever I want, and I always get what I want. Get that through your thick cabeza." He paused and looked around at them. "What's so interesting? What are you all looking at down there?"

"Nothing," Juan replied.

"Yeah, nothing," cried Henry.

"Let me see," Monty shouted as he shoved his way to the center of the circle and gazed down.

"It's a praying mantis. Don't hurt it," cried one of the girls.

Monty sneered as he looked down at the insect. "What's it praying to?"

"That's just what it's called. It's a bug. It doesn't really pray," Henry blurted out. He didn't say the rest of what he was thinking, which was, "How stupid can you be?"

Monty stood there with his arms crossed. "It wouldn't

matter if it did. There is no such thing as God, anyway."

Henry stood up. "That's not true! You shouldn't say that."

Monty picked up the bug. "Here, I'll prove it to you."

The group of kids gasped simultaneously. "Please don't hurt it," came cries from the group.

"OK, Henry, pray to God that this praying mantis doesn't die in the next minute. If it's still alive, then there is a God. If it dies, then there isn't."

Henry looked at Monty with terror and disgust. "Put it down. Don't be a jerk."

Monty made the motion with his other hand as though he was going to smash the insect. "You better start praying. I'm counting down. If you're not praying out loud by the time I get to one, the bug dies, and it will be your fault. Five, four, three, two..."

"OK, OK," Henry said as he started to pray. "Our Father, who art in heaven, hallowed be Thy name. Thy kingdom come, Thy will be done, on earth as it is in heaven."

"OK, that's enough," Monty instructed. "Now let's see what happens."

Everyone was motionless and stared at Monty as he held the insect in his hand. Then Monty smiled. "You dweebs, I was just kidding." He put the insect gently on the ground. There was a collective sigh of relief. Then Monty crushed it with the heel of his shoe.

"See, I told you, Henrico stupido. It wouldn't matter how hard you prayed – ha ha ha ha." Monty was hysterical with laughter. Some of the girls were crying. Everybody was upset.

"And if any of you go blabbing to Ms. Arnold, I will step on you. Just try me. It will be so much fun, for me that is, not for you. You'll be in pain." With that, he turned, jumped the fence and then turned back toward them. He continued walking backwards while pointing at the group and roaring with laughter. As he turned again to see where he was going, he walked straight into a pole. When they saw this, the kids stood up and pointed as they roared with laughter.

"Yes!" Henry yelled, and gave Juan a high five.

Dazed for a moment, Monty turned and saw the group pointing and laughing at him. He felt the surge of pain from the lump that was starting to form in the middle of his forehead. He touched it and cringed, "Ouch!" Embarrassed, and with a painful bump on his head, he turned to run across the street. He was not paying attention to the traffic because he was still a bit stunned from what had happened. Monty did not see the car that had just made the yellow light and was speeding his way. He started to cross the street, and a loud honk pierced his ears. He froze and looked at the oncoming vehicle. Suddenly, he was yanked out of its path. Monty quickly turned to see who had pulled him back.

"Son, you should be more careful. That car is a lot bigger than you. Why, you could have been squashed like a bug," said the old black gentleman standing beside him.

Monty was speechless. He just stood there staring at the man who had just saved his life.

"You with me, son?" the man asked. Monty gave a strong yank and ripped his arm away from the man's grip and walked away. "You might want to thank the Lord that you weren't killed," the old gentleman said as he stood watching Monty cross the street. He shook his head and murmured, "You're welcome."

After Monty reached the other side, he turned to the stranger and flipped him the bird.

Back in the classroom, everyone took their seats. When Monty came strolling in, a few of the children started to giggle. Monty looked around, gave them a dirty look, and sat down.

Juan chuckled and looked over to Henry, who had a big grin on his face. Monty glared at Juan, giving him the evil eye.

"OK, boys and girls, this afternoon we will announce the winner of our Easter photo contest. Your assignment, as part of our culture and customs class, was to take a picture that is representative of Easter. We will use these photos as a way to learn a little bit about this particular holiday."

Juan sat there, lost in his own thoughts. He was out of the running and would get a failing grade on this assignment. Juan didn't know that this would be the last time he would see Monty McPride for a long time. Blake McPride had paid the crew overtime and added more men to get their house finished several weeks early. The trucks were moving the McPride household as the children at PS 189 sat in Ms. Arnold's class that very afternoon.

Blake McPride would be sending the car around after school to pick Monty up and take him to their new home in the most exclusive neighborhood in Cary. Monty would start class at the prestigious McGuire Academy the following day. Juan would come across Monty again in the future, but their encounter would be much worse.

Ms. Arnold read the names of the winners for best photos. "We will start with third place; the winner, Katherine Smith. Second place goes to Laura Diaz. All of your photos were quite good, and it was difficult to select the top three winners, but there was one photograph that the judges felt deserved first place, and the winner is Monty McPride." The class reluctantly applauded as Monty held his head high.

Diogenes Ruiz

4

Twenty Five Years Later

There was applause from around the room and the man in his late thirties stood with his head held high. He seemed to be thoroughly enjoying the somewhat subdued applause. It was a formal black-tie affair and members of the Board of Directors of McPride Industries and their families were in attendance. Some faces had expressions of surprise. Others murmured at their tables. The applause died down quickly, and Monty McPride spoke to the crowd.

"Thank you, thank you very much. I've worked hard for this, and I am as surprised as some of you to receive the top sales award for this past year. Since there are so many products here at McPride Industries, I tried a new strategy this year so that I could reach more customers with more of our products. Well, it seems to have worked. Thank you again." Polite applause arose then subsided quickly.

The wait staff took their cue. Now that the award had been presented, they started to serve dinner. Background music from the jazz trio softly filled the room. The 300 people gathered at this year's banquet started the evening by watching a video about the company. Then they heard from key department heads about the company's growth overseas and the role of technology within their new products division. This was followed by award presentations to individuals in separate categories. Now that the awards were out of the way, the guests were free to converse and dine. Next, they would hear from the CEO about something big that was on the horizon for McPride Industries.

Monty's award was a bit of a surprise to everyone, including the folks organizing the event. At the last minute, Fred Wilkins explained to Beth Avery, the event coordinator, that there was an error in the name of the designated recipient. A new plaque was produced within hours of the event.

Harold Jacobson could not hide his disappointment when Fred Wilkins informed him of the error and the fact that he would not be receiving the sales award after all. As everybody started to eat, the chatter level increased in the hall.

"Malarkey!" whispered one of the guests to others at his table.

"Idiots!" Tom Harris, the director of human resources was not pleased. "That guy hasn't worked a day in his life. If it weren't for his rich old man, he'd probably be out on the street or in jail. He must think we're all a bunch of idiots." Tom knew that Monty was the least likely candidate to receive any kind of award, especially one that was dependent on hard work.

Tom chuckled. "Oh my, I don't know how he did it, but I think most folks recognized that there is one big smelly elephant in the room."

A few of the guests congratulated Monty and shook his hand as he made his way from the stage back to his table. He walked by Blake McPride's table with his head held high. He glanced over at his father. Blake McPride did not say a word.

John Delmont, senior advisor to the CEO and a strong voice on the board of directors, turned to Blake. "Wasn't Harold Jacobson supposed to receive that award?"

After the Monty peacock had strutted past their table, Blake turned to John and nodded. "Yes, Harold Jacobson was supposed to receive it. I'm not sure what just happened, but, oh, how I wish it were true, John. Nothing would make me prouder. Lord knows, I've given Monty every opportunity to earn an honest living here. I felt I owed him that much. After all, he is my son."

Blake paused and glanced at Monty's table, where he seemed to be engaged in animated storytelling with the guests. "I know that is a poor excuse, John."

"This is a big company, Blake, but you can't continue to

sponsor ineptness, incompetence, and pure…" John hesitated.

Blake wanted to hear the rest of what he had to say. "Go ahead, John, you've always spoken your mind. Don't stop now."

John looked Blake McPride in the eye and reluctantly finished his sentence. "Pure…" There was another pause. "Disregard for others."

John Delmont did not say what was really on his mind, what he really wanted to say about Monty because he could not bring himself to say it. Even though Blake McPride trusted him and encouraged him to speak freely, John could not tell his boss that he thought his son was "pure evil." Blake was the father, after all, and as much as John felt he could speak openly, this was a line he did not want to cross.

"Perhaps I shouldn't say this, Blake, but you need to stop feeling guilty for whatever it is you think you did or didn't do and exercise some tough love. Stop feeling like you owe him everything, because the cost just keeps rising, and I'm not just talking about the money. You're lucky to be alive, my friend. You've had your run-in with stress and fortunately that medicine you take every day is keeping you alive. Monty's effect on morale is becoming worse, and I'd hate to see something happen to you because you are trying to rid your guilt by catering to Monty. You cannot take responsibility for Monty's decisions."

Blake nodded. "You're right, John. I've been trying to make up for my own incompetency as a father. I've moved Monty to just about every division within the company, and the result has always been chaos. This is terribly difficult, John, but I think I know what I have to do. God help me and forgive me, but I may have to fire my own son. I'm not sure how he hoodwinked this award, but I'll get to the bottom of it."

A little while later, Blake McPride excused himself from the table and went up on the stage to deliver his big announcement.

"Dear friends and colleagues, I want to take a few moments to share some exciting news. Some of you may have heard rumors that we have been testing a new secret product. Well, it's true. It's been in the works for quite awhile, but I think we are close to a breakthrough. We are about to make medical history in the treatment of burns. Now, to tell you a little bit more about this incredible technology, here is Ray Cromwell, with MedezTeck

Labs. He is heading up our research efforts."

Ray Cromwell took the stage and shook Blake McPride's hand. Ray's brown hair was neatly cut, and his face was pleasant in the way he seemed to exude confidence. His smile was sincere, and he did not appear to be nervous, although he was very nervous. This was the most exciting project Ray had ever worked on. He had always dreamed that he might lead a team in a breakthrough project like this and at 34 he was getting his big chance.

Ray had attended North Carolina State University and was an avid basketball fan. He had a great deal of charm without any self-centeredness or conceit. It was his love of basketball and his honest charm that helped him meet and win the heart of his true love. It happened one day while at a big rivalry game between NC State and the University of North Carolina Chapel Hill. He was dressed in his NC State red enjoying the game on his side of the stadium among a sea of fellow classmates all in red. After the second quarter, he visited the concession stand to get a beverage. The line behind him soon swelled with fans dressed in red. All of a sudden, a girl dressed in UNC blue approached the concession stand and the reds started booing. This was no ordinary rivalry.

The young lady was surprised by all the attention and booing she was receiving. When Ray Cromwell took a look at Angie Arias, his heart skipped a beat, and he emotionally switched sides. UNC blue had never looked this good. She was the most beautiful girl he had ever seen. He told the person in line behind him to save his place. Then he stepped out of the line, waved his arms at the reds and said, "It's OK! She's with me!" He winked at her, held out his arm in a true gentlemanly fashion and escorted her to his spot at the front of the line, as roars of "Traitor! You rat! It won't last! You're crazy!" came from the rest of the line.

She was special and Ray was still an avid NC State fan. Contrary to what his friends said to him when he fell for a UNC girl, there was no therapy needed in the household of two people who loved each other and loved hating each other's team. It made for some interesting commentary during rival games.

Now on the stage, ready to take the microphone, Ray's personal game was on. He introduced himself and began his presentation.

"Ladies and gentleman, BD109 is a revolutionary product

that allows the various layers of thermal tissue to bond at an extraordinary rate. It is absorbed by the skin rapidly and begins bonding cells and tissue almost instantaneously. It is conductive and facilitates the formation of skin. One of the extraordinary properties of BD109 is its ability to bond with inorganic tissue to create a new type of epidermal system. We have had success with different medical fabrics and created artificial skin prototypes. The implications are far reaching. Our testing is in its final phase, and there should be more good news regarding the outcomes later next week. We expect that the McPride Industries Bonding Agent, BD109, will cut the recovery time for burn victims in half."

There were spontaneous murmurs throughout the audience and heads were nodding. Eyebrows were going up everywhere, including Monty's.

5

The Devil's Apprentice

Fred Wilkins wanted power, prestige and wealth. He knew he would get it the day McPride, Jr. took over the company. Fred also knew that Monty needed his help to get what he wanted. Since Fred was the leading geek at McPride Industries, he had access to all the company's computer systems and the data they contained. He was an expert programmer, hacker and sleaze bag.

Both men sat in Monty's office the following day. "Good job, Wilkins. I don't know if those idiots, including my father, actually bought it, but things went smoothly yesterday. Are you sure no one can track what we did and find out how we altered the numbers?" Before Wilkins could respond, Monty cut him off. "Doesn't matter, by the time they figure out how we did it, I'll be running this place. By then, it won't matter."

Wilkins responded with confidence. "No one will ever be able to track anything. It's amazing what you can do with a little programming know-how and a few well-placed bugs. Money skimmed here, money skimmed there, along with the commissions from the sales you never made, the dollars become quite significant after you add..."

Monty cut him off again. "What did you find out about this bonding agent?"

"It's just like Ray Cromwell said. It will revolutionize medicine, but here, take a look at this." Wilkins produced a large brown envelope and handed it to Monty. "It's a report on BD109 that I managed to retrieve from the MedezTeck Lab's server. I think you might be interested in the results."

Monty glanced at the report and gazed at a series of numbers and charts, none of which made much sense to him.

"So what? All I see are a bunch of charts. Why are you wasting my time with this, Wilkins?" Monty had a short fuse, especially when it came to geeks and their techno-babble.

Wilkins waved his finger at the report. "Look at the toxicology section on page 16."

Monty turned to page 16 and looked it over. Then he took a deep breath and looked at Wilkins. "More gibberish and charts, Wilkins, just tell me what I'm looking at before I bitch slap you."

Wilkins finger pointing became frenzied as it pointed to a small chart which had several items listed with numbers scaling from 1 to 10. He looked like a kid who found a golden ticket in a chocolate bar. "Do you see that chart? It refers to the level of user dependency that is a projected outcome from BD109 if repeatedly ingested. Basically, it means that in addition to being an externally applied bonding agent, BD109 has the potential to be the most addictive drug on the planet. However, it is not being formulated for internal use. It's intended for external application only, in which case it would be harmless."

Monty grabbed the chart and stared at it. He turned to his partner in crime. "Wilkins, if you weren't so damned ugly, I'd kiss you."

"I thought you would be pleased"

"Pleased? Hell, this is the best news I've had since I learned that the old geezer will die without that medicine he takes! By the way, is everything ready?"

"You bet!"

"Who would have guessed that we could make a fortune treating the burnies and another fortune supplying the druggies." Burnies is what Monty decided that he would call burn victims. He thought of it right then and there, spontaneously. He thought himself to be quite witty. Witty, spontaneous and fun, that was Monty. He also considered himself extremely good looking. Whenever Monty saw another man he thought might be attractive, he would rate himself in comparison. He always won, of course. He was absolutely sure that there was no one more witty, spontaneous, fun or handsome than he. What a delight he was to himself, convinced that people perceived him as breath of fresh air in their otherwise drab world.

"So, Wilkins, when will the bonding agent by ready?"

"Ray Cromwell's report suggests that if the final test is successful, BD109 should be ready for manufacturing in less than three months." Wilkins was satisfied that he had earned big brownie points with the future CEO of McPride Industries. He was climbing the corporate ladder faster than Superman could leap a tall building in a single bound.

Monty reclined in his seat with his hands behind his head as he stared up at the ceiling. Then he quickly spun around in the chair. After all this good news, he was feeling just a little bit giddy, and that brought out the fun and spontaneous side of him. All of a sudden, Monty dipped his hand into the candy bowl on his desk and flipped something to Wilkins.

"Here, have a mini Easter egg. I love Easter, don't you, Fred?" Whenever Monty was in a particularly good mood, feeling all giddy and spontaneous, he would refer to Wilkins by his first name. Otherwise, it was always "Wilkins."

Monty continued in his euphoric bliss. "I just love Easter. It's the season for marshmallow bunnies and chocolate-covered eggs. It's the best time of the year, don't you think, Fred? Christmas is overrated, too commercial, kind of phony. You know what I mean?"

Diogenes Ruiz

6

Father's Keeper?

Blake McPride spent most of the morning in meetings with the heads of marketing and public relations. They reviewed ideas for BD109 product names, and discussed strategies for a public relations campaign. Two of the top choices for product names were Epiphoenix and DermalNew. That afternoon, Blake planned to review another important project for Broadwell Medical. He buzzed Ms. Simmons.

"Peggy, is the Broadwell documentation complete?"

"No sir, but I am close to finishing and should have it for you in a half hour or so. Will that be acceptable, Mr. McPride?"

"Yes, that's fine, Peggy, and I need you to pick up a refill of my prescription. I seem to have misplaced the bottle and shouldn't be skipping it for two days."

Peggy Simmons was Blake McPride's personal secretary, going on three years. She had run out to get his prescription before, but she did not like it when he skipped taking it for whatever the reason. It seemed to be happening frequently. He kept misplacing his bottle. She planned to call his doctor for an extra prescription to keep on hand, in case he lost his medicine again.

Peggy would not have to worry about that because there would not be a next time.

She hoped that he was not starting to get senile. "Yes, sir. Would you like for me to run out, right now, to have it refilled?"

"No, no, that won't be necessary. I've done it before, and

I'll probably do it again. I hate being ball-and-chained to a prescription. Finish what you're working on first. I'll be fine."

Peggy did not insist, although she was tempted. "Yes, Mr. McPride. Will that be all?"

Blake McPride was a good employer, and he appreciated the work performed by his staff. "Yes, Peggy, thank you."

"You're welcome, sir." She immediately returned to her work on the Broadwell Medical file.

Blake reviewed the marketing plan and product names for BD109 again and decided that he liked "DermalNew" better than "Epiphoenix," which sounded too contrived for his taste. As he reviewed the marketing schedule, he heard a knock on his door. Blake looked up and saw a head poking in, which he ignored. He turned his attention back to the document on his desk. Monty opened the door the rest of the way and let himself in. He took a leisurely stroll over to the guest chair. On his way, he looked around the chairman's office. As he did so, he puffed up his chest and wore a grin on his face. He slowly sat down and patiently waited to hear his father say something.

Monty sat quietly continuing to gaze around the office. He was in no hurry. He amused himself by thinking of the Rolling Stones song, *Time is on My Side. Yes, it is.*

"If you're waiting for me to congratulate you, you can forget it." Blake McPride's voice was low and matter-of-fact. He continued to examine his papers.

Monty smiled and began making his case. "Oh, come on, Dad, I've been working really hard." He said these words without much conviction, like someone reading a script but not doing a very good job at it.

Blake gave him a quick glance. "You've never worked hard at anything in your entire life."

Monty spoke, but it still sounded like bad acting. Even the words he used were a little odd for a grown man. "Gee whiz, Dad, isn't that kind of harsh? I mean, after all, I did win the sales award." Monty liked saying, "Gee whiz." It was another spontaneous bit of retro awesomeness. He even made it sound a little nasal just for effect.

The chairman looked up. "That's just it. You've never even been on the map. Your sales efforts have been nonexistent, and the only reason you're here is because you are my incompetent son." The old man's blood was beginning to boil.

Monty, now sounding a little more serious, continued his defense. "I've changed, Dad, really. I wanted to show you, so I worked really hard and it paid off. I won top honors."

The old man looked up. "This sudden quest to show me that you've changed wouldn't have anything to do with the fact that I'm retiring and will be naming a successor soon, would it?"

Monty put on his best polite and sincere voice. "I realized that it would be up to me to lead this company someday. Your retirement has forced me to see what a fool I've been not to work harder, but, I am determined to work as hard as necessary after you retire so that I can lead this company to greater profitability."

It sounded so rehearsed and artificial that the chairman just rolled his eyes. He looked at Monty for a long moment, expecting to hear more dribble. *"I guess that's all he rehearsed,"* the chairman thought.

"You can cut the act, Monty, I'm naming Stevens as the new chairman, and I've decided to redistribute ownership of this company among the board and the employees. These people have worked hard and sacrificed much to get us where we are today. Consider your small but significant equity share an act of charity, because you sure don't deserve it."

Monty quit his good boy act and got in the chairman's face. "You mean you'd cut your own son out of the chairman's position for some stranger?"

Now Blake McPride's blood was boiling. "You're unqualified, dishonest and have never worked at anything in your life. Nothing!"

Monty knew it was true. However, that was not a good enough reason for his father to select Stevens over his own son. "Even when I did something to make you proud, you'd never admit it. As a kid, when I won that photography contest, you never congratulated me or said that you were proud."

"Good grief, you lunatic, that's because you didn't win it. You stole that photo from the Arias boy. Do you think I didn't know? Do you think people are stupid? Heaven help me, but I should have put my foot down, after first giving you a good kick in the ass. All that childhood nonsense that I thought you would outgrow has only gotten worse. I always thought you'd turn around and be an honorable man. Heaven knows, I've tried. You've never gone without. You've always had it easy, too easy, and that's my fault. Look at you, a grown man, and you still don't know what it is to work for something you want. You think that you can scheme, weasel or bully your way into getting it! Someday you really will get what you deserve. Unfortunately, so will I for not doing a better job of instilling a good set of values and a proper ethic into you. I should have listened to your mother, God rest her soul. She warned me about overcompensating for my frequent absences by giving you everything you ever wanted and not being stricter with your sorry ass. God help me and may your mother forgive me, but you're fired, you ungrateful brat!"

"Fired?" Monty snickered. "You're right, old man. We each get what we deserve, except your son who's getting screwed by his own flesh and blood." Monty took his seat and looked rather relaxed. Blake McPride, on the other hand, did not look too good. He was flushed, and his heart was beating a mile a minute.

Monty sat for a moment and observed the chairman. "You know, you don't look well. Have you been getting enough sleep?"

Blake McPride was breathing a little harder now as he looked up at Monty. "If you think that your fake concern for my health is going to change anything, you have another think coming to you."

Monty sat patiently. "You're wrong, old man. My concern is quite genuine." He looked at his watch, then thought about what colors he might choose for the office walls. "Say, isn't it time for your medicine, you know, the stuff that's keeping you alive?"

The chairman gave a piercing glance to his son. "What did you do with my pills?"

"Now, now, old timer, take it easy. I found them on the floor. You must have dropped them. Say, you're kind of overdue to take them, aren't you? That's not good." Monty held the small pill bottle in his hand and examined the label as though he had all the time in the world. He listened to *Time is on My Side* playing in his head and a grin came across his face.

"OK, Monty, give me the pills and get out of here." Blake hoped that his son would be reasonable, especially since breathing was becoming increasingly difficult. Monty continued his casual examination of the medicine's label. Then he put the little plastic bottle back in his pocket, took out a piece of paper and slowly unfolded it. He took a pen from his shirt pocket, removed the cap and tested its ability to write on the papers sitting on the chairman's desk. He made a few scribbles, and then drew a happy face, but instead of a smile, he made a wiggly line.

"Sure, old man, as soon as you sign this executive order naming me your successor."

Blake McPride was now beginning to feel dizzy. "Monty, I never thought you could stoop so low. I don't have time for this, and you leave me no choice but to call security." Thank God for the panic button on the side of his desk. Blake never thought he'd have to use it, but this was now a life-and-death situation. *"How could my own son do this?"* Shock, grief and pain crossed through Blake's mind as he pressed the silent alarm button under his desk.

Monty produced a nail file and started to file the nails on his left hand. He did one, blew the dust off and started to file the next one. "I took the liberty of disconnecting your little buzzer so we won't be interrupted, and you don't have any meetings this afternoon, so we have plenty of time to take care of our little business."

"Hiding my medicine, Monty? My God, boy!" The chairman's voice sounded a bit raspy now, as though he needed to drink some water. "You've crossed the line. You're mad." Monty was now filing his right hand.

"And you're dying," Monty replied as though he were commenting on the weather.

Blake reached for the phone. Monty grabbed it. The old man's hands began to tremble. Pain ran up and down his left arm. His chest tightened. He struggled to get the phone again but Monty applied more force. Blake McPride was dying. He knew he had very little time; he tried to scream. Monty put his hand over his father's mouth and took out a handkerchief from his pocket. He then stuffed it into the old man's mouth. Monty grabbed Blake's face, looked into his fading eyes. "OK, old man, this is your last chance to be a good boy." Monty then put the pen in Blake McPride's hand and signed the chairman's signature with it. He had been practicing. The old man was weak, and it was easy to make the swirly signature which looked like a doctor's illegible scribble.

When Monty released his grip, Blake McPride collapsed onto the floor. He was barely conscious and tried to say something but could not because he was gagging with the handkerchief stuck in his mouth. Monty looked down on his father, calmly put the signed executive order in his jacket pocket, collected his pen, and got down so he could try to hear what the old man's last words would be. He removed the handkerchief from the chairman's mouth and leaned close. "What is it, old geezer?" Before he could utter a sound, Blake McPride closed his eyes. At that instant, the office door behind him opened, and Peggy Simmons walked in with the Broadwell files.

She screamed, "Oh, God, what happened?" as she ran over to Blake.

Monty was leaning over him and quickly wiped his own face with the saliva-soaked handkerchief. He looked at Peggy and cried like a baby, saying to her with squinty wet eyes, "I don't know. He just collapsed. I tried to revive him, but nothing worked."

Peggy kept her cool and asked, "Did you call 911?"

Monty leaned over his father's body and sobbed.

Peggy dialed 911 as Monty gave a master class performance on sobbing. Peggy did as instructed by the 911 operator. She put her phone down and kept the connection open. Then she gently pushed the sobbing Monty out of the way. "Here, let me help. You go sit down." She then applied CPR while staying on the line with 911. After what seemed like an eternity, the paramedics finally arrived. As they took Blake down to the ambulance, Monty made the most of his dramatic acting and continued to sob and shake his head.

Peggy provided a copy of the prescription to one of the paramedics. "I was just about to go down and have this refilled. He misplaced his medicine again. It's happened several times."

Monty overheard this and blurted out, "Again?" He turned and joined the conversation. "I told him to keep that medicine safe. I knew something was wrong when he started to look red and then, (dramatic pause) he started to gasp. I looked all over his desk because I suspected as much. Then (another inspired dramatic pause) he just collapsed." Monty's brilliant acting was in high gear as he clutched the paramedic by the shirt. "You have to save him.

He is the only thing that matters to me."

The paramedic looked at Monty with understanding eyes. "Take it easy, sir." Then he took Monty's hands and gently removed them from his shirt collar. "We'll do everything possible, I assure you."

Monty drove to the hospital. He thought about going to Hooters. Getting the old geezer to sign the executive order had made him hungry. He decided that he would continue his loving son routine until the old man was certainly dead. Then in his spontaneous brilliance, he imagined the Munchkins from the *Wizard of Oz* singing, *"Ding Dong the Blake is Dead,"* as they danced around the old man's bed. There would be a blanket over the body with just the feet sticking out. Around the big toe, there would be a tag. "The Blake is dead," would be written in big bold letters.

He went to the emergency entrance and was instructed to wait in the lobby until the doctor had something to report. Monty sat patiently waiting and fantasizing about how he would redecorate his new office.

A few moments later, Peggy Simmons, John Delmont, and several others from McPride Industries arrived. John Delmont headed straight for Monty. "What happened?"

Monty paused and breathed deeply, as though he was in pain. He let out a deep sigh, and with his best "Can't you see I'm hurting?" face, he looked at John. "We were in his office, when he started to gasp. Then he collapsed. Ms. Simmons entered at that moment. Thank God for her. I was beside myself."

John looked Monty over and thought, *"Yeah, I bet you were."* "What were you doing in Blake's office?"

Monty looked at John with and expression of utter disbelief. "What do you mean, what was I doing in his office? I was talking with him. What else would I be doing? He wanted to see me."

John didn't trust Monty as far as he could throw him. He had a bad feeling about this. "What did he want to see you about?"

"What are you, a drill sergeant?" Monty blurted in a hurt voice. Then he struggled hard to try to make himself teary eyed. "He called me in to congratulate me and to discuss my promotion." John's eyes nearly popped out of his head. He was a short man, just five feet two inches tall. He was stocky and at this very instant he felt like ripping Monty's head off. He knew that was a lie. Blake McPride was not planning to congratulate his grown demon child. In fact, he was sure that Blake was thinking of cutting the kid loose. "What?" John roared. "You've got to be kidding me. If you think I'm going to...."

Monty turned away as John was in mid-sentence and ran toward the doctor, who had come out to inform the group on Blake's condition. With a dramatic look worthy of an Academy Award, he asked, "How is he, Doctor?" He clasped his hands together as if praying that it would be good news. You'd think Monty was a regular actor on a Spanish tele-novela. The type where somebody always cries as they get their dramatic close up.

Dr. Bryant began to explain the situation. "Well, Mr. McPride..."

Deep inside Monty's head, he felt giddy. He was just called Mr. McPride by the doctor. The others also heard it. He was going to be the one they turned to for leadership. He would occupy the big chair from which he was almost cheated by the greedy old buzzard. His performance was going so well. He zoned back in and listened to what the doctor was saying.

"Your father has suffered a severe trauma, and it seems he did not take his medicine." The doctor paused and took Monty by the elbow and led him down the hall, just far enough so that he could deliver the bad news in private.

"He's in a vegetative state, Mr. McPride. I'm sorry, and I have to tell you that the odds of him recovering are not good."

That was Monty's cue for more melodrama. He raised his voice so everyone could hear his distress. "What do you mean, not good? Is there any chance that he'll recover?" The rest of the staff members in the lobby quickly approached. They were now standing behind Monty.

All were listening to what the doctor was saying. "He is and will continue to be in a vegetative state. Short of a miracle, I'm afraid your father is going to spend the rest of his life, whatever is left of it, needing round-the-clock care. But there's more, I'm afraid. I would not be surprised if he doesn't recognize you or know who he is. He might also hallucinate. His trauma was quite severe. He can't speak. He can barely move, and he is very weak."

The doctor paused after realizing he just delivered quite a bit of bad news. *Maybe it would have been more merciful if Blake McPride had passed away quietly on his way to the hospital,* thought the doctor. Finally, he turned to Monty and everyone in the group. "I'm very sorry. I wish I had better news."

Monty put on the saddest face he could conjure before he looked in the direction of the group of employees. Then he turned back to the doctor. He lowered his head and slumped his shoulders. "Thank you, doctor."

The Doctor gently placed his hand on Monty's shoulder. "You can visit him in the morning. I'll call you if there is even the slightest change in his condition."

Monty nodded and stood there with his head hung low. *"I'm brilliant,"* he thought.

Dr. Bryant removed his comforting hand from the shoulder of a dejected Monty. "We'll do everything we can, Mr. McPride." Then he went back to tend to his other patients.

Everyone left the hospital waiting room quietly, each with their own sorrow and distress over what had just happened, all except Monty. He was thinking of how much he felt like Gene Kelly in *Singing in the Rain*. *"What a wonderful feeling, I'm happy again."* He could hear the tune in his head. *"Do do doo do do do do do do doo do."*

John Delmont had other thoughts. He knew that Monty was lying about why he visited Blake McPride's office. John decided that he would change his schedule tomorrow. He had a meeting in the morning, which he could not cancel. It would not take more than an hour. He would cancel the rest of his appointments and devote the remainder of the day to doing his own bit of investigating, with a little help from a friend. He knew just the person to call. It was a buddy from his military days. They had served together, and his friend had opened a private investigation firm.

John felt that he owed it to Blake to get to the bottom of this. Not only was Blake his boss, but he was a good friend. John had watched as Monty wreaked havoc throughout the different departments at McPride Industries. If Monty had anything to do with Blake being in this sorry condition, John was determined to find out.

Unfortunately, John Delmont would never get a chance to start his investigation.

7

Juan's Recruitment

Ray Cromwell walked into Juan's work area and smiled when he saw his brother-in-law.

"Hi, Juan, I've got a favor to ask."

Juan Arias sat at his cubicle at Blanderdan and Associates developing diagnostic software for their server clients. Juan hated to admit it, but as it turned out, he followed his father's advice and became a computer programmer. It was a job. He didn't love it, but it paid the bills. He still enjoyed photography but did less of it over the years. Real life seemed to have gotten in the way and zapped his dreams of becoming a photographer. He would occasionally leafed through a copy of *National Geographic*.

After college, Juan married Leigh, a woman he met at a wine tasting party. He was not much of a wine drinker and didn't fancy himself as a wine expert. Leigh knew a great deal about wine and somehow they hit it off. They've been married for two years. The fire is gone now, but they seem to be content with being comfortable in the marriage.

Juan wished he could have the kind of relationship that Ray and Angie enjoyed, with two great kids, David, age 5, and Matthew, age 3. Children would be nice, but Leigh was not ready for kids just yet. He wondered if she would ever be. He loved his nephews and spent as much time as he could with them. Leigh was lukewarm as an aunt. Juan was glad that his little sister found someone that made her happy. They attend church regularly with the kids, something Juan never had growing up. Juan attended Mass with them occasionally. After his marriage to Leigh, he has not attended. She never cared much for it and considered it a waste of a perfectly good hour.

Juan looked up and gave a smile to his brother-in-law. "What's up, Ray? What's this favor you need?"

"Well," Ray began in his best *Mission Impossible* voice, "your mission, should you decide to accept it, is full of excitement, danger, suspense and chocolate-covered eggs. If you are caught, the government will disavow any knowledge of your actions." Then he paused and in his ordinary voice said, "I need you to be the Easter Bunny."

Juan was amused by the request. "Are you kidding, Ray?"

Ray glanced at the shopping bag he was holding. "No, I'm not kidding, partner. I already rented the costume. This year we invited some friends, and we plan to have an Easter egg hunt and make it special for the kids."

Ray did not hear an immediate yes from Juan, so he added, "It was Angie's idea."

Juan chuckled. "Oh yeah, and just because it was Angie's idea you think I will automatically agree to it?"

Ray came clean. "Actually, it was my idea but Angie thought it was great. She's all for it. I thought David and Matthew would enjoy it, especially if their favorite uncle shows up as the Easter Bunny." Ray paused. "You know you want to do it. I can see it in your eyes."

"Why is it that whenever you want to get me to do something, you always play the David and Matthew card?"

"Because it always works, besides, I know how crazy you are about the kids."

"Why don't you do it, Ray?"

Ray extended his left arm, made a clenched fist, and in his Darth Vader voice said, "It is your destiny, Juan." Ray did not know just how prophetic those words would turn out to be.

"Well, I can't. I'm going to be out of town," Juan replied in a dead pan voice.

"Really, Juan?" Ray was genuinely disappointed.

Juan then cut the act. "What time do you want me to be there? I couldn't say yes too fast. You would think I'm easy."

Ray laughed. "That's because you are."

"I'm not easy," Juan insisted. "More like a pushover. There's a difference. Now, give me the costume and get out of here before you talk me into dressing up as the tooth fairy."

Ray handed over the bag and gave Juan a brotherly hug. "Thanks, brother."

"Give the kids a hug for me." Juan sat down to resume his work, but before getting back into his project, he yelled to Ray, "Tell Angie that the Easter Bunny expects his very own pack of Peeps, and they have to be the yellow ones. Any other color will be a violation of Easter Bunny protocol." Ray waved his hand in acknowledgment and left the office.

8

BD109

Ray entered the MedezTeck Lab building. Today was the big day for the final test results of the BD109 bonding agent. If successful, the approval from the governing agencies would be imminent. He would stop by his office first to check his messages and drop off the large pack of yellow Peeps. Then he would head downstairs to the lab.

The first voicemail message was from a copier sales guy trying to get an appointment. At once, Ray hit delete. The next one was from KC Mitchell, a colleague who was working on the BD109 project with him. *"Hey Ray, sorry that you have to work with that lunatic at McPride Industries. I just called to give you a little advice: you'd better watch your back."*

Ray thought that to be a strange message. He didn't understand why KC would refer to Blake McPride as a lunatic. He was a great guy; he went out of his way to be polite. As far as Ray knew, Blake McPride was a demanding but reasonable man. Lunatic was not a word that he would have used to describe him. His son was another story.

He then played the third message. *"Hello Ray, this is Peggy Simmons at McPride Industries. I just wanted to inform you that Blake McPride is in the hospital and will not be meeting with you next week as planned. Instead, you will be meeting with Mr. Monty McPride, our new acting CEO. You may remember him from last week's awards banquet. If you have any questions, please feel free to contact me."* There was a pause. *"It doesn't look good, Ray."*

Ray sat back in shock. *"You can't be serious. How can they possibly put that lunatic in charge?"* Ray spent enough time at McPride Industries to know more than he cared to about Monty. This was bad news indeed. Ray genuinely liked Blake. He would have to find out what happened and send his best wishes for a speedy recovery.

Ray had experienced several run-ins with the infamous Monty and was not looking forward to working with him. The most recent encounter occurred two days before the awards banquet. Ray was in the lobby and saw Monty speaking to the Spanish cleaning man about the men's bathroom being a mess.

"Messy, muy messy. Comprende?" Monty spoke loud and repeated his words slower and louder "Meessyy, mucho mucho meessyy." Then he put his hand to his ear in an exaggerated motion. "Can you hear me, do you understand – comprende?" He was talking to the man as though he had a hearing problem, which he did not. Then Monty pointed at his Rolex and said, "Today!" Then he made a shooing motion as though trying to get rid of a dog. The man simply replied, "Yes, sir," and headed toward the men's bathroom. Monty rolled his eyes and made a comment loud enough so everyone could hear, "Why don't these people speak English like everybody else? I hope he can mop better than he talks!"

Ray's first encounter with Monty had taken place six months earlier. The meeting with Blake McPride had gone well, and Ray was preparing to meet another client for lunch. On his way out of the bathroom, as he cracked the door, he glanced at Monty standing beside one of the administrative assistants' desk. It happened very fast, but Ray thought he saw Monty McPride deposit a large wad of spit into the admin's coffee cup and put it back on her desk. He noticed that Monty was about to turn around and scan the area. No doubt he had scanned it before making his move and now needed to verify that no one had seen him. Ray immediately looked down and walked straight out of the bathroom without so much as glancing in Monty's direction, but he knew something was terribly wrong with this individual.

Instead of heading to his lunch appointment, Ray made his way to an inconspicuous spot and pretended to be checking his text messages. He approached the admin's desk, still pretending to be preoccupied with his messages. Monty was still standing by her desk. She handed Monty a batch of papers, and he said, "Thanks, Latisha." The young, attractive black woman smiled and replied, "You're very welcome, Monty."

The admin picked up her coffee cup. She smiled again at Monty as he stood there staring at her. She started to bring the coffee cup to her lips.

"Excuse me," Ray blurted out as he arrived at her desk just as she was about to take a sip of the spit infested coffee. The young lady looked up with surprise as she put her coffee cup back down. Monty looked over at Ray with shock and anger. Ignoring Monty altogether, Ray addressed the young woman. "I'm so sorry to interrupt you," he said as he came around to the coffee cup side of her desk.

"Andrea, is that you?" Ray asked with surprise. "I was just on my way out when I thought I recognized you. Do you remember me? It's Ray!"

She gave him a bewildered look. "Andrea? My name is not Andrea. It's Latisha, Latisha Jones. You must have me mistaken with someone else."

Ray froze and a look of embarrassment beamed across his face. He looked at Monty, then back at Latisha. "Oh my, this is embarrassing. You look just like a dear friend. I was sure it was you. I was so happy to see you. Please excuse me." Ray shifted his phone and the briefcase which he was holding awkwardly. He then fumbled and knocked the contaminated coffee over, being careful to bump it so that it fell onto the floor.

"Oh geez, I'm terribly sorry," Ray gasped. "I'm such a klutz. That's what I get for being in a hurry. Here, let me help you clean that up."

The young woman stood up from her chair. "Please, don't worry about it, sir. I'll have someone from our cleaning crew take care of that."

Ray faced Latisha and extended a handshake to her. "Please, excuse my clumsiness. I should be more careful."

"Don't let it trouble you, no harm done. At least it didn't get all over my clothes." Ray smiled and turned to Monty, whom he had not yet officially met. "I'm sorry for the mishap. Please excuse me." As Ray turned to leave, he heard Monty speak.

"Do you know who I am?"

Ray turned back. "No, I don't believe I've had the pleasure. I'm Ray Cromwell." Ray held out his hand to shake Monty's.

Monty did not take it. His hands remained folded across his chest. In a voice overflowing with condescension, he said. "I am Monty McPride of McPride Industries. What is your business here?"

Ray looked at the pompous ass of a man, who no doubt got some strange pleasure out of spitting into unsuspecting people's coffee cups and then watching them drink it. "I had a meeting with Mr. Blake McPride, the CEO, on a project and was just on my way out."

"I know he is the CEO. Do you think I'm an idiot?"

Ray apologetically replied, "Oh no, sir, I didn't mean..."

Monty cut him off. "What were you meeting with him about?" He maintained his stern and demanding posture.

"I came to provide information."

Monty gave Ray a "you must be kidding" look. "That tells me absolutely nothing. If I wanted useless information, I'd read the Bible. What was the meeting about? I need you to be more specific."

By this point, Ray didn't think that Monty was an idiot. He knew that idiot was too kind a word. This guy was much worse. Ray paused before responding. He didn't need to give this bully any information about his business with Blake McPride. "I'm not at liberty to discuss my business with Mr. McPride, unless it is with Mr. Blake McPride." Ray responded with a more confident and less frenzied demeanor than he had exhibited after spilling the coffee.

Monty stared at Ray. He was upset that someone had ruined his fun. He was hiding his anger and was puffed up like a peacock. "Blake McPride is my father. Any business you have with him, you have with me. So, I'll ask you one more time. What was your meeting about?"

Ray replied in a polite but stern tone. "I'm sorry, Mr. McPride, but I am not at liberty to discuss it. Now, if you'll excuse me."

With that Ray turned to leave.

Monty snickered, "You should be more careful, Mr. Cromwell. Someone could get seriously hurt by a spilled cup of coffee."

Ray continued walking and did not respond. Monty studied Ray as he walked away.

As soon as Ray was outside the building, he dialed McPride Industries. "Please connect me with Ms. Latisha Jones. This is an emergency. It's her dog sitter calling."

The pleasant young woman came on the line. *"This is Latisha Jones, I don't have a..."*

Before she could say another word, Ray cut in. He used as good a fake voice as he could muster so that she would not recognize him. "This is important, please listen. I was in the building just before that nut knocked over your coffee. I'm glad he did because the other guy standing by your desk put a large loogie in it."

"A what?"

"Spit! He spit in your coffee while you were turned, and he put it back on your desk very quickly and neatly. I don't think anybody saw him, but I did. I was just about to warn you when that guy bumped it off your desk. You might want to be careful around that Monty. He's a creep. Keep your coffee cup where you can see it if he happens to come by, and just be on your guard with him. Who knows what else he might try?"

Before she could respond, Ray hung up. Then he called his lunch appointment and informed them that he was running late.

Ray had stayed clear of the younger McPride. He had never brought it up with Blake because he did not want to open a can of worms. If Monty wanted to find out what was discussed at the BD109 meeting, he could go straight to his father.

Diogenes Ruiz

9

Good News Bad News

Ray got up from his desk and headed downstairs to the lab. KC Mitchell was already there waiting for him with a grin on his face. "What's so funny, KC?" Ray was not in a good mood and the thought of having to meet with Monty McPride gave him the creeps.

KC extended his hand and grabbed Ray's to shake it. "Well, Ray, it's been a long journey, but we've finally done it." KC was in charge of conducting BD109 tests. "This formulation bonded instantly and held with all skin types and even some fabrics." KC became increasingly excited as he delivered the news. "Do you realize what this means?" he asked. Then he answered his own question. "We are about to revolutionize medicine. We are making history!"

Ray gave KC a halfhearted smile. "Yeah, that's great. Too bad the old man won't get a chance to see it. It makes me sick to think that his good-for-nothing son is running the company now."

"We'll have an investment stampede. Monty will get run over by it. Have you ever been in an investment stampede, Ray? I've personally never experienced one, but I hear they are quite beautiful. The investors run hysterically towards you, like orangutans in heat, waving wads of million dollar bills." KC acted out his impression of an investor orangutan walking around waving his arms.

"I hope you're right, KC."

"Of course, I'm right. Any investment the company goes after will be in the bag. We might not even need it."

As Ray put his briefcase on the desk, he gave KC a concerned look. "I'm not talking about your investment stampede," he said as he placed one of the small vials containing the final BD109 formula into his briefcase.

"What then?" asked KC.

Ray grabbed his briefcase. As he was closing it, he turned to KC. "I hope you're right about Monty getting run over." He thought for a moment. "Who else knows about the success of this test?"

"Just you and me right now."

"Great, let's keep it that way for the time being OK?"

KC nodded. "Sure, OK. So, you're not going to tell Monty?"

Ray thought about his upcoming meeting. He paused and looked at KC. "When you have a meeting with the devil the last thing you want to do is give him more fuel for his fire."

Ray arrived home, eager to hug his wife and kids. It had been a long day. He was glad that Angie had decided to put her teaching career on hold to be home with the children.

"Honey, I'm home!" David and Matthew ran to greet their dad and give him a hug.

Angie was in the kitchen preparing dinner. She liked her role as a stay-at-home mom. Housekeeper, she thought, was not such a bad title. It had gotten a bad rap. She was the keeper of her home, her kids, and her husband. She was content and did not feel the least bit guilty about not working outside the home. Fortunately, Ray's income was sufficient to keep their modest finances in order. They lived in an unassuming split level home. Angie drove her minivan and Ray drove his fuel efficient sedan.

Ray walked into the kitchen and gave his wife a hug from behind and a peck on the cheek as she was stirring the pot of chili.

"Hmmm, smells good."

Angie turned and smiled. "I'm glad you're home, Ray."

"Yeah, me too." He took a deep breath and let it out slowly. "It's been a long week."

Angie tasted the chili and added a touch of pepper. "So,

how's the formulation going?"

"It looks as though it will work." Ray put his briefcase down on the counter that connected the kitchen with the family room. It was his little nook. He opened his briefcase and held up the small sample of BD109. "Look."

Angie turned and glanced at the vial he was holding. "What is that, food coloring?"

Ray examined the vial, "I guess it does sort of look like that. This is it, Angie, BD109, the stuff that McPride Industries hired us to formulate. It's amazing stuff, literally bonds organic fabric with human skin. There will be lots of uses for this and big changes in some medical treatments."

"That's great, honey." Angie listened, but her attention shifted to things that needed to get done around the house. "Ray, you need to help me get this place ready for the Easter party on Sunday."

"Say, Angie, you'll never guess who I got to be the Easter Bunny."

"Juan," she replied, matter-of-factly.

Ray pretended to be surprised that she knew. "How did you know?"

She smiled. "You always rope him into helping you with things you don't like to do. But what I want to know is if you got permission from the real Easter Bunny to have Juan impersonate him. He is very particular you know."

Ray thought Angie's smile could melt any man's heart. He felt lucky to have such a great wife. He was starting to feel better from the stress of the day. "The Easter Bunny and I go way back."

A little while later, the Cromwells sat down to have dinner. Ray couldn't wait to tell the kids about the Easter party. "Are you guys excited about Easter this Sunday?"

Little Matthew shrugged his shoulders as he shoved food into his mouth.

His older brother David reported on his day at school. "Ms. Clare is teaching us about Easter. She says Jesus rose from the dead after they killed him. He was hung on a cross. They put nails into his hands and feet, and there was blood all over the place. They were really big ones, but first they beat him and did stuff to him. They tortured him, and then they crucified him. She said that they killed him on a Friday, and he got up and came back to life on Sunday." David held up three fingers. "That's three days later, Easter Sunday that he got up, and people didn't believe it. Some of them wanted proof, and he let one of them stick his finger in his side." Matthew made a poking motion with his hand. "But, there were still a lot of people who did not want to believe it."

"Did Ms. Clare say why they killed him?" Ray asked.

David continued with his mouth full of food.

Angie shook her head. "David, swallow your food. Don't talk with your mouth full."

David swallowed and took a drink from his cup of grape juice. He now had a purple mustache. He continued, "Ms. Clare said that Jesus died so that everybody has a chance to go to heaven when they die. And get this," David said enthusiastically. "Jesus didn't even hurt anybody, he didn't do anything wrong. She said that some of the people in charge back then were jealous and afraid of Jesus. They even let a bad guy go, and the guy in charge, Pompous Pilot, handed Jesus over to be killed."

"That's Pontius Pilate," Angie corrected, "not Pompous Pilot."

"Yeah, that's the guy," replied David as he dug back into his dinner.

After swallowing his food and another sip of grape juice, David asked, "Why did God let Jesus die? Ms. Clare said that Jesus was the son of God. Couldn't he have saved him? God can do anything, right?"

Angie and Ray looked at each other, and after a moment, Angie responded. "That's why Easter is special. God could have saved his Son, but he let Jesus die. He sacrificed his only Son so that we all have a chance to go to heaven, just like Ms. Clare said."

Matthew looked up and had a question of his own. "Did Jesus have a pet rabbit? Is that the Easter Bunny?"

Angie turned to him. "I don't know if Jesus ever had a pet rabbit, but the Easter Bunny came later as a way to help us celebrate what Jesus did for us. Easter is not about the Easter Bunny. It's about the risen Jesus. The Easter Bunny helps us to celebrate that."

Ray chimed in. "As a matter of fact, I think the Easter Bunny might be coming here on Sunday, after Mass." David and

Matthew both looked at each other and made cheering gestures.

10

Leigh

Juan's wife, Leigh, could be described as a little self-absorbed. Well, maybe more than a little. Tonight she sat in front of her vanity pampering herself. She worked hard to maintain her good looks. "I can't believe my eyelashes aren't longer," she yelled out to Juan as she looked in the mirror "Everyone in my family has longer eyelashes than me. It's not fair." She let out a sigh. "Juan, can you get me a glass of wine? I'm so exhausted."

"Sure, honey," was Juan's standard response.

Leigh was always exhausted. She worked thirty hours a week and acted as if she worked sixty hours.

"Juan, have you seen my tweezers? I need to pluck my eyebrows. You didn't borrow them, did you?"

"Nope, I'm letting my eyebrows grow nice and bushy. Then I'll set them on fire and dance for you."

Leigh laughed, "You crazy teddy bear." That was her pet name for him. She had a thing for pet names. She also had a tendency to overly demonstrate affection when in social situations with Juan. Most people witnessing this would feel the urge to vomit. Her group of shallow, pretentious wine snob friends thought it was cute. They got together every month for wine tasting parties. The next one would be their turn to host.

"Hey, bubs," that was her other pet name for Juan. "Aren't you going to get a haircut before the party?"

Juan thought for a moment. *What party?* Then before

she could reply, he muttered to himself, "Oh crap!" He knew what party but had forgotten about it.

"Oh, Juan, you silly goose, the wine tasting party on Sunday. I'm going to show off my new wine glasses and everybody will probably want me to tell my funny stories. You didn't forget, did you?"

Juan's mind was dreading the inevitable. "Well, actually, something came up." He said it and waited for Krakatoa to blow. A few seconds later, it did.

"What do you mean something came up!" Leigh yelled, upset that he had forgotten such an important event.

"Something came up. I'm sorry, dear."

"What do you mean something came up?" she roared back.

Destined to suffer Leigh's wrath, he knew he'd better come clean and get this over with. "Honey, I'm sorry, but I can't be here for the party. I have to be the Easter Bunny for the kiddy party at my sister's. I promised Ray I would do it."

Leigh was not at all interested in his commitment to entertain his nephews and their bratty little friends. She wanted Juan at the wine tasting party, which took place every month at a different person's house. Who else was going to help serve the wine and help her with the party? "You're always helping him with some dumb thing or other. Call him up right now and tell him you can't do it, that you had a previous commitment with your wife. He'll understand, and even if he doesn't, you need to be here on Sunday."

"Yes, honey, but I can't back out now."

Leigh was now furious. She was used to getting her way. Every once in a while when she was upset she would stamp her feet and yell at Juan. This was one of those times. She marched in and demanded, "Now, you call that Ray and tell him that you can't be his stupid rabbit this year."

Juan didn't respond immediately. He looked down and then back up at her after a moment's pause. "You're right. It really isn't fair that I leave you all alone with the wine tasting club and have all the attention on your shoulders. They won't leave you alone wanting to hear you talk about yourself and tell your funny stories, and I won't be here to interrupt and help. All the attention will be on you. That's just not fair. Maybe I should call Ray and tell him that I can't make it."

Leigh was going to have a successful party one way or the other. Maybe she could get Bill Fletcher to be her errand boy for the evening. She knew that good old Bill would do anything for her. It might not be so bad to have the stage all to herself. She was the life of the party. Maybe everyone would have a better time if she did it solo. Juan's jokes were stale, and he was not really into the wine tasting as she was. His palate was quite unsophisticated; beer was his beverage of choice. Maybe this was a blessing in disguise, and she would not have to hear him talk about how boring it was to listen to people talk about wine minutia, as he called it.

"Well, maybe I'm being selfish, honey. You go and play Easter rabbit with the kiddies, and I'll just have to tough it out. They are your sister's kids, after all." Leigh seemed calm and thoughtful.

"Are you sure, dear?" Juan needed to get a confirmation on her verdict.

"Yeah, go ahead, and say hello to the little brats for me." Leigh thought how glad she was that she didn't have kids.

Sunday finally arrived. The Cromwells attended the 11:30 a.m. Mass at St. Paul's. After Mass, people hung around greeting one another and catching up. Today was no different, and there were a lot of kids at Mass. It was Easter and Fr. Carl's homily was as much for the kids as it was for the adults. He talked about "the gift." That's what he called Jesus' sacrifice on the cross. He said it was a gift to all, even to those who did not choose to accept it. It was there nonetheless. He encouraged everyone to accept the gift of forgiveness of sin and new eternal life which was freely given. It was a beautiful and inspiring homily.

The Cromwells got home at 2:45 p.m. They were hoping to be home a little earlier since the party was supposed to start at three. With all the chatting after Mass and their stop for a quick bite, it had gotten late. It was almost time for the party. Tom and Jane Clymer, their next door neighbors, and Wilma Evans, the elderly neighbor who lived a few houses down, arrived early just as the family pulled into the driveway. They came to help with the last minute preparations. Tom and Jane had a little girl, Hanna, age

3, and a little boy Chase, age 6. They were expecting their third child. Jane was due to deliver in a couple of weeks. She looked as though she was going to pop any minute. The children got busy playing in the backyard and Wilma came in and began to get the kitchen ready.

"You don't have to do that, Wilma," Angie cried. "I'll set everything up after I change. It will only take a minute."

Wilma was a take charge kind of gal. "Don't you worry, hon. I may be old, but I can manage quite well, no worries. I'll just start organizing things a wee bit for when the kiddies get here. I'll make sure that everything is safe. With all the little ones that will be here today, you can't be too careful, you know."

Angie smiled. "OK, but just don't work too hard. I want you to have a good time and enjoy your grandchildren when they get here."

Wilma replied with her well-meaning "get out of here, I've got it covered" wave. She was one of the original homeowners in the subdivision. She was a great neighbor and always kept an eye on her neighbors' homes when they were away. You just never knew when someone might try to break in. As a result, she knew everything about everyone. She was the matriarch of the neighborhood. Everyone knew Wilma and, although she was a bit quirky in her way of seeing danger in the most harmless things, she was always willing to lend a hand, even when you didn't really need one or want one.

Angie disappeared to the bedroom to change. Matthew and Chase went out to play in the backyard, and the two younger children, David and Hanna, were in the family room coloring. Little David was making a card for Hanna. He planned to marry her when he grew up.

Jane sat on the sofa next to the two young children. "Wilma, I wish I could help you but, well, I'm just not up to being on my feet right now."

Wilma gave her the wave from the kitchen. "Hush, you don't need to be helping, just sit quietly and relax yourself. You got that little one in the oven. I can handle things."

Jane smiled and closed her eyes to relax for a bit until the party officially started. She had staked out the most comfortable place to sit.

Ray and Tom headed to the garage and took out the batch of plastic multicolored Easter eggs which they hid in different areas of the front of the house. The strategy was to make them easy enough to find, but not too obvious. There was an art to hiding Easter eggs and the men conferred and went about it as only men would do. Of course, there had to be one or two eggs with a high difficulty factor to find. This was insurance just in case they got one of those greedy, slightly older kids who wanted to do an Easter egg shut out.

Wilma got busy in the kitchen getting out the paper plates and plastic forks. She placed the Easter egg dye vials in a neat group toward the side, off the pass-through counter, next to Ray's briefcase.

For an old woman, she worked at a blazing speed, like someone had set a timer and she was trying to beat the clock. She set out napkins. She even secured the toaster's wall plug, which looked as if it was about to fall out. She found the disinfecting wipes and started wiping down the counter, which she might have thought to do first. Wilma, the cleaning tornado, wiped down the refrigerator handle, the cabinet handles and, in her final victory wipe of the counter, she knocked over the food coloring dye vials along with Ray's briefcase onto the family room side of the counter. The contents spilled onto the carpeted floor.

Jane opened her eyes "Here, I'll get that."

Wilma quickly cut her off with a shake of her finger. "You'll do no such thing, missy. You stay. I got it." Jane did not argue. She closed her eyes again. Wilma hurried around, out of the kitchen, to pick up the spilled contents. As she made her way around, one of two remaining food coloring dye vials rolled off the counter and into the side flap of Ray's briefcase.

Wilma quickly made it to the other side of the counter and picked up the papers which had fallen into three piles, along with a couple of pens, a small calculator and a pair of reading glasses, all of which were scattered on the floor. Fortunately, the briefcase fell with its lid open, and it was right side up, a lucky break. Nothing was broken. It was an easy task as she put all of Ray's items back, all except one. She closed the briefcase and set it neatly on the computer desk next to the counter. Then she picked up the remaining vials of food coloring and put them in a neat little group back on the counter.

Angie came back into the family room and caught site of the pregnant woman whose eyes were closed. "Are you OK, Jane?"

"Yeah, I'm just taking it easy before the rest of the kids get here."

Wonder Woman Wilma waved a hand. "I told her to take it easy. She doesn't need to push herself."

Angie looked over to the kitchen side with the neat collection of food coloring vials, the paper plates and plastic forks. "Wow, that looks neat. Thank you, Wilma. Now why don't you come over here and sit with Jane."

"What about the eggs? Aren't you going to boil some so the kids can color them?" Wilma sounded as though there was an impending egg emergency.

"They're all done. I'll take them out of the fridge in just a little while. Now come on."

Wilma reluctantly came over and sat down in one of the family room chairs. She looked nervously at her watch. "Wasn't he supposed to be here by now?"

Angie glanced at the clock on the wall. "Yes, it's just three o'clock now. He should be here any minute."

"Does Juan have any experience with kids?"

Angie was a patient woman, but Wilma had a way of making even the most patient person wish they could remote control her mouth. "He'll do OK, Wilma. Don't worry."

Just then, the door opened, and Ray and Tom walked in with a stream of kids and guests. Some of the children ran to the back yard to play. A few of the others joined David and Hanna as they colored. Ray put on *"Willy Wonka and the Chocolate Factory"* for the kids, and the Easter party was officially underway. Now all that was needed was for the Easter Bunny to make his grand entrance.

Wilma's grandchildren had not arrived yet. She stepped over to the window and glanced up at the sky. She approached Ray, who was pouring sodas and setting up some snacks for the kids. "Is your home properly grounded in the event of a lightning strike?"

Ray stopped pouring and looked at Wilma. He pictured the

old woman assisting Dr. Frankenstein, waiting for lightning to strike. "Wilma, it's perfectly sunny outside. There is no chance for rain today. Why do you ask?"

"You can't be too careful, you know."

The front door opened, and Wilma's daughter and her grandchildren entered the house. Wilma headed straight for them. She would check the children for fractured heads, bleeding ears or other visible signs of the apocalypse before saying hello.

Diogenes Ruiz

11

Duty Calls

The car zooming down the highway was a regular compact car, only this one had a giant rabbit behind the wheel, and it was in a hurry. Juan got stuck doing cleaning duty before Leigh's wine-tasting party. It was scheduled to start early in the afternoon. Leigh invited a few of her girlfriends over. They would have a little fashion and makeup get together, followed by the wine tasting later. Then she would have dinner delivered.

She could not simply have a wine tasting party like everyone else. She had to outdo everyone. There was no such thing as a simple anything for Leigh. Everything had a way of escalating into a big production, including the side effects of work. She was not simply tired after a thirty-hour work week. She was exhaaauuusted and she wanted you to know it. She was a one-up expert. Regardless of your story, she had a better one and she delivered it through an affected accent with a heaping of condescension and a nasal twang.

After cleaning the house because Leigh was simply too exhausted, Juan got into the rabbit costume. He would have just enough time to get to Ray and Angie's house on time, maybe a few minutes late. He would have to push it.

Other than the man in the rabbit suit sweating profusely because he was running late, and the rabbit ears sticking out from the opened sunroof, it was just another car on the highway. That is until he passed a hidden police vehicle while doing 78 on a 65 mile per hour stretch of Interstate 40.

Juan passed several cars and decided to get into the right hand lane, that's when he saw the flashing blue light behind him. "Oh crap, I don't need this right now. Not now!" He pounded the steering wheel and mumbled unpleasantries at the police officer in pursuit. He optimistically kept his speed below 65, hoping that the police car would pass him and chase a real criminal, but no such luck today. The police car was on his tail. Then the siren made a creepy howling sound which meant "pull over."

Juan looked in the mirror as he watched the police officer take his time getting ready to get out of the cruiser. It felt as though he had been sitting there for a half hour. "What was he doing in there?" Juan wondered. Could he be finishing a crossword puzzle, or maybe he was crocheting a sweater? It just made no sense to pull someone over and then make them wait that long, especially when they were late for an Easter party. Two minutes after pulling Juan over, the police officer got out of his vehicle and slowly approached Juan's car.

As the officer approached, he looked inside the rear passenger seat of Juan's rabbit mobile. Then he stopped and gazed at Juan for a moment. The officer was tall. He wore sunglasses. He was chewing gum discreetly, or it could have been tobacco. "License, please," he said to the man in the bunny suit. The officer took the license and examined the photo. Then, he studied Juan. He looked back and forth from Juan to the license several times as though he had all the time in the world.

"Sir, are you carrying drugs, weapons or contraband in your vehicle?"

Juan wondered what kind of drugs or weapons were usually carried by a rabbit. Maybe some catnip-spiked carrots, a set of carrot-ended nun-chucks, and possibly some rabbit nudie magazines. "No, sir, I'm not carrying any of those items. I'm on my way to a kid's party; I'm running late. I didn't want to disappoint those terrific little youngsters," Juan responded with a big phony smile.

The officer did not respond.

"You understand, don't you, officer? I didn't mean to go too fast. I promise I'll slow down. I just didn't want to be late."

After a couple of discreet chews on his gum, the officer

took another look at the license and said, "I'm letting you off with a warning this time."

Juan could not believe his ears. *This must be my lucky day.* He would soon learn that he was mistaken. At least for now, he could get on his way.

The trooper handed the driver's license back to him. "Keep it under the speed limit. Don't be a foolish wabbit."

Juan thought he heard the police officer say, "Wabbit."

"Did you say wabbit?" Juan asked.

The trooper began to chew less discretely. "I did! What about it?" The trooper asked in a slightly agitated voice.

Juan sank down a little bit lower behind the steering wheel. "No, nothing, I didn't know..." The trooper was now chewing less discreetly. There was a definite increase in chewing activity going on. "You didn't know what?" the trooper demanded, slightly raising his voice. Now his jawbone looked a little tense.

Juan reluctantly finished his sentence in a low voice as he shrunk further into his seat. "I didn't know grown policemen said wabbit, that's all."

The cop was now chomping on his gum or whatever it was. He could chew wood with that jaw. "And what's wrong with me saying wabbit?" the cop demanded. This time, he leaned in toward Juan with one hand on his gun. Juan sank further and further into his seat.

"I asked you a question. What's wrong with me saying wabbit?" The trooper asked a second time. He chewed so hard, Juan thought the cop could have chewed the tires of his car.

Juan was desperate to get his foot out of his mouth. "No, no, nothing's wrong with you saying wabbit. I didn't mean..."

"Sir, I need you to get out of the car," the trooper said in a stern voice.

Juan was now panicking "But, officer, I didn't mean anything..."

"Get out of the car, NOW!" came the booming voice of officer Lockjaw.

Wilma looked at the clock and went over to Ray.

"Do you think he had a horrific car crash? What do you think is keeping him?"

"I don't know, Wilma. I tried his cell phone but got his voicemail."

Wilma thought for a moment. "I hope he didn't have an aneurism while driving."

Ray looked at the old woman. "What makes you say that?"

"It's been known to happen. It's one possibility. And, if he didn't fasten his seatbelt, he could be thrown from his vehicle. Did you know that a person can be projected over twenty feet if the car is moving at sixty miles per hour?"

Ray tried not to let Wilma drive him crazy. "He's OK, Wilma. If something happened that prevented him from being here, Juan would have called."

"Not if he's dead," she countered.

"He's not dead. He's just late. It could be traffic or a number of other things. I want you to relax and think positively, Wilma. He's all right. You'll see."

Wilma sighed. "Well, OK. I just hope he has Easter Bunny insurance. You know, like Elvis insurance. Those men that impersonate Elvis have Elvis insurance."

Ray found it amazing how a person could create so many worrisome scenarios. Didn't she have enough crap to worry about, without creating all of these fantastic scenarios in her head? He knew that Wilma was a widow. Ray wondered whatever happened to Mr. Wilma. How could somebody live with a mega worrywart like that?

"Why would anyone need Elvis insurance?" Ray asked, knowing that he would regret it.

"Why, they could have an accident and fall on their guitars. They could get impaled. It could get wedged in their abdomen or rib cage."

Ray wished he had a clapper and that it could shut Wilma up with a simple clap. "OK, Wilma. Look, why don't you go and make sure the kids have plenty to do until he gets here. I'm sure Juan will be here shortly." He continued to talk as he guided Wilma to where the kids were coloring and playing. Then he stopped and said, "He's OK, I promise. He'll spend a couple of hours with the kids. He is trustworthy, and we're all here. What can possibly go wrong? Now relax, OK?"

Wilma reluctantly went to the kitchen to find something to

organize. She wasn't in the mood to play with kids right now. She had some more worrying to do. She thought of several ways in which Juan could have an accident which resulted in the loss of his head. Maybe he failed to stop and ran into the back of a flatbed tow truck. Just as she was running beheading scenarios, the Easter Bunny walked through the front door.

12

The Easter Bunny Arrives

Angie was standing by the door as Juan came in. "Thank goodness you're here. The kids are waiting for you." She grabbed Juan's hand and dragged him to where the kids were waiting. "Look boys and girls, the Easter Bunny is here!" The children screamed with excitement.

Juan was dying of thirst after his ordeal getting to the party, so he knew just how to start things off.

"Why don't we have something refreshing to drink?" the giant Easter Bunny asked the children. A collective "Yeah" rang out. "Let's see. What should we have?" He saw Ray point at the large pitcher of lemonade.

"How about some refreshing lemonade?"

The chorus of kids agreed. "Can we color our lemonade?" one of them cried out. "Pleeease?" Then they all chimed in and said, "pleeease."

Juan held up his bunny hands. "OK, I think that's a fine idea."

Little Johnny, one of the two brats in the group, didn't much care for the idea. "I don't like lemonade, and I don't like the Easter Bunny either."

Johnny's mother overheard this from the living room. She came into the kitchen. "Johnny, you had better be nice, or you're going to be in big trouble, and I mean it, mister!" Johnny dragged himself over to the kitchen table and sat down.

Juan then continued, "Let's gather around and have a colorful lemonade drink. This is going to be fun." Juan led the kids into the large eat-in kitchen. He set his keys down on the counter.

As the rest of the children gathered around the table, little Johnny decided he would sit by himself at the pass-through counter. He didn't want any of this baby stuff.

Wilma organized the clear plastic cups around the table. She took the food coloring vials and put them in the center. The children gathered around. Angie filled the cups with lemonade and Wilma passed them out.

All of the children tried to grab a color vial. Some wanted the same color. The Easter Bunny acted as the food color vial dispatcher. They each got whatever color Juan handed to them. "They're all magic colors, so it doesn't matter which color you get."

There was a lot of chatter coming from the living room as Ray, Tom and the other adults talked and munched on snacks. The Easter party was off to a fine start. Jane had not gone into labor. The kids were getting along, for the most part. All the eggs outside were successfully hidden. Juan was doing a fine job as the Easter Bunny, and Wilma didn't have to worry about Juan being beheaded in a car accident.

Johnny sat at the counter idly playing with Juan's keys. When everyone, except Johnny, had their lemonade and food coloring, Juan said, "OK, let's color our lemonade! Let's do it at the same time and see all the colors. Then we can drink it."

The children eagerly took their food coloring vials and put a few drops into their glasses. The Easter Bunny provided his expert consultation for best results. "Just a few drops kids. You can start with that and add a little more to make it darker. Don't add too much or it may get too dark."

As the group was busy coloring their lemonade, oohs and aahs began to fill the room.

The children wanted to see what colors their friends had and compare it with their own. There were red, blue, yellow, orange, and lime-colored lemonades. Juan began putting in a few drops from his food coloring vial but it came out in a stream. "Whoops! That was a lot more than I meant to put in." He stirred the coloring into his lemonade. As the children saw Juan's glass turn a bright green, they collectively oohed and aahed.

"Wow, that's cool," one child said.

Another pointed. "That's a cool green."

Then Juan held up his glass and said, "Cheers." Some of the children mimicked his actions, and they all drank.

Juan was parched and the radioactive-looking green lemonade tasted delicious.

"Can we do it again?" shouted one of the children.

"What a fine idea. Sure," he replied, in a jolly Easter Bunny voice.

The kids laughed, and Wilma replenished the lemonade. One of the kids accidentally spilled his cup. Wilma became panic stricken when she realized that she had failed to anticipate having a roll of paper towels on the table. "Angie, where do you keep the extra rolls of paper towels?"

"They're in the pantry, in the hallway that goes to the garage."

Wilma disappeared in a flash to get the paper towels.

"Hey, Easter Bunny, I want my own lemonade," little Johnny demanded.

Juan gestured, "OK, come on down and join us at the table."

Little Johnny twirled the car keys. He smiled at Juan, held his keys up and dropped them into the toaster.

"You little brat," Juan murmured as he went to the counter to get his keys out of the toaster. He picked up the toaster and turned it upside down. Nothing came out. He jiggled it. Still nothing came out. He put it back down then walked to the other end of the counter and unplugged it. He needed something that he could use to pry the keys out. He found a kitchen knife in the utensils drawer.

Juan instructed the kids to go ahead and color their lemonade, which they did. Little Johnny wanted the same cool color of lemonade that Juan had. So he took Juan's food coloring vial and tried putting it in his lemonade, but the vial was empty. He reached for another color vial from the unused bunch that remained at the center of the table.

Meanwhile, Juan pried the toaster with the kitchen knife. *"Almost got it, just a little further."*

Wilma came in with the roll of paper towels. The first thing she noticed was the plug which had obviously fallen out. She shook her head and murmured. "You can't be too careful." The second thing she saw, after she inserted the plug into the wall, was a convulsing man-rabbit being electrocuted.

Juan, who was finally about to dislodge his keys, felt a jolt run through his body. He sounded as though he was choking. The children looked up at the Easter Bunny doing a strange and wild dance. They stared in shock as Juan's body jerked out of control. Everyone in the living room sprang up and ran to the kitchen. Wilma finally realized that it would be a good idea to pull the plug out of the wall, but she could not pull it out fast enough. There was a zap and loud pop. Juan's body collapsed as though someone had sucked every bit of energy out of it. He hit the floor. There was a clash as the toaster followed. It crashed to the tiled kitchen floor pulled down by Juan's hand, which was still in it. The car keys landed to the side of the toaster along with the kitchen knife. There was a gasp from everyone in the house. Then there was complete silence. It was broken by little Johnny: "The Easter Bunny is dead!"

13

Diagnosis: RABBIT

Juan was unconscious but miraculously still alive as the ambulance raced to the hospital. His pulse was weak. The paramedics unzipped the rabbit costume then they hooked him up to a monitor. They arrived at the hospital and rolled the gurney in.

People in the waiting area and the staff behind the service desk looked on as the man in the rabbit costume was rushed through the doors and down the corridor. The paramedics cautioned people standing in their path. "Emergency! Coming through!" At once, people stood to the side and let them pass.

One little boy in the lobby looked on with an expression of concern. He glanced up at his mother as he noticed the large bunny feet sticking out and the set of rabbit ears.

Juan disappeared through the set of double doors and into the operating room. As soon as they were inside, one of the doctors stepped up. "OK, let's get him on the table and see what's going on."

One of the paramedics looked puzzled. "We have him hooked to the portable monitor, but it isn't picking up much. His heart seems to be beating, and he seems to be breathing, but according to these other readings, he should be dead. We are getting no other vitals. We thought one of the monitors was malfunctioning, so we tried the other and got the same results."

The doctors on call rushed to try to stabilize Juan.

"I think he's going into synaptic shock," yelled one of the

doctors.

"This doesn't look good," said the other.

"This makes no sense, but there must be a way to stabilize him. Why is his pulse getting weaker?" asked the nurse.

"I think we're going to lose him," cried another nurse.

"C'mon people, let's figure this out!" shouted the lead physician.

The intense blurriness began to fade as Juan tried to focus his eyes. He was groggy for a few moments. Eventually, he was able to make out the two faces looking at him. He didn't recognize either of them. He cleared his throat. "What happened?"

One of the nurses turned to the other. "He seems OK."

"Good, here's his wife," said the other nurse as Leigh came into the room. "We'll leave you alone now. The doctor will be here shortly."

Leigh went to the side of the bed as the two nurses exited the room. "Ray called me and told me you had an accident and that it was serious. What happened? How do you feel?"

"I feel fine. The last thing I remember is trying to get my keys out of the toaster. Suddenly, I got a wallop of a shock."

Leigh looked at Juan. "So, you're not dead or anything. You look ridiculous in that dumb costume, but otherwise you're OK?"

"Yeah, I'm OK. I felt a little groggy before, but there's nothing wrong with me."

Leigh rolled her eyes. "Great, Juan. I get a call telling me that you could be dead. I have to leave the wine tasting party, which was going so well. I was in the middle of my story about the time I picked up the wrong case of chardonnay. I rush down here like a lunatic to find that you're really quite all right? I mean, I'm glad you're all right, but the timing could not have been worse. It won't be our turn to host a party for another year."

Just as Leigh finished her whining, there was a polite knock on the hospital room door. A man opened it slowly and poked his head in. "May I come in?"

Leigh turned around to look at the man. "Yeah, come in, doc."

He stepped into the room, and one of the nurses that had

been there earlier was with him. "Hello, I'm Doctor Rashad, and this is Nurse Betty." He turned to the nurse. "Will you take Mrs. Arias to the waiting room while I speak with Mr. Arias?"

Juan thought that this well-meaning doctor didn't have to be so concerned with privacy. After all, Leigh was his wife, and he was sure his insurance card was valid. He had coverage. "That's not necessary, doc. Leigh can stay."

The doctor looked at Juan with a polite smile. "Mr. Arias, I really think it would be best to have your wife wait in the other room while we talk."

Juan was now sure that this was not about his insurance card. The only reason to have a private conversation, as far as Juan could see, was to tell him that he was going to die or had cancer or something. Juan started to get scared. "What's going on, doc? Why do you want her to leave? I'd like her to stay. Is something wrong?"

Dr. Rashad smiled and then gave a polite little wave. "I just thought it might be best, but never mind. Your wife can stay if you'd like. I don't want this to be any more stressful than it already is. You're both going to have to work through this together, anyway."

Leigh's ears perked up. "Work through what? I feel fine. He's the one that got electrocuted."

"And I feel fine," Juan added.

Leigh sat in the visitor's chair next to the bed. Dr. Rashad pulled up his stool and sat by the side of the bed so he could address both of them. "Mr. Arias, you've had an incredibly bizarre accident. I have never seen anything like it before."

Juan was anxious and wanted this polite man, whom he guessed was from India because of his accent and complexion, to get to the point. "That's just great, doc, but just tell me what's going on so I can get out of this stupid costume and go home." Juan sat up and started to unzip the costume.

Dr. Rashad, quickly but gently, stopped Juan's hand from undoing the zipper. "Please, Mr. Arias, you don't want to do that." He paused for a moment and then continued. "Unfortunately, it's not that simple. Let me explain. We removed the costume when you were admitted, but we had to put it back on." The doctor searched for the right words.

"You see, Mr. Arias, not only were you electrocuted, which affected your body's neural pathways, but you also ingested a substance. I think Mr. Cromwell referred to it as 'a bonding agent,' which has altered your body's chemistry. I'm afraid that somehow the shock your body suffered, along with your ingestion of the bonding agent, has somehow produced a state of neural pathway displacement."

Juan looked at Leigh, then back at Dr. Rashad. "What does all that mumbo jumbo mean, doc?"

"When you were admitted, we removed the rabbit suit to do some scans and monitor your vitals. Soon afterwards, your body went into synaptic shock. We ran several tests, but the results were always the same. If you are out of that rabbit outfit for more than a three-minute period, you will go into synaptic shock and die. It took us awhile to figure it out, and, fortunately, we did manage to figure it out just in time. We thought we were going to lose you there for a while. The scans reveal that the synaptic pathways in your body have somehow been turned off. The fabric pathways in your costume are functioning as neural transmission pathways. In other words, Mr. Arias, that rabbit costume is keeping you alive. Without it, your body cannot send the necessary signals throughout your body."

Juan sneered. "Come on, Doc, you've got to be kidding me. I mean, that's good, and you kept a straight face as you told that story. It sounds like something on *Star Trek*. Did Ray put you up to this? What a sick sense of humor. That's the last time I let him talk me into one of his crazy favors."

Dr. Rashad looked down for a moment and then looked at Leigh and back at Juan. "No, Mr. Arias, this is not a joke, and your brother-in-law did not put me up to this. I can assure you that what I am telling you is fact." He thought for a moment and then continued. "You are fortunate in one respect."

Juan wondered if Dr Rashad had turned into Pollyanna. There was nothing fortunate about this.

"How's that?"

"My theory, Mr. Arias, is that when you ingested the bonding chemical agent, which you thought was food coloring for your lemonade, it created a kind of alternate electrical pathway outside your body through the fabric in the costume."

Dr. Rashad turned to Nurse Betty. "Please bring me the game from the children's examining room." The nurse quickly ran out.

"This is ridiculous, Doc," Leigh said. "How could something like this really happen?" Just then the nurse returned with what the doctor requested.

Dr. Rashad held up the *Operation* board game to demonstrate his theory. "The game is relatively simple. It consists of a game board with a drawing of the patient lying on an operation table. There are little cavities where organs are located. For example, there is a little cavity for a funny bone, appendix, heart, et cetera. They are all located in their correct anatomical position. The object of the game is to remove one of the organs with a small pair of tweezers. If you are not careful, and the tweezers touch the sides of the cavity containing the organ, the red light bulb located on the patient's nose, goes off and there is a loud buzzing sound. It signifies that the organ was not removed successfully, besides scaring the player to death. The player that is able to remove the most organs successfully without triggering the red nose buzzer is the winner."

"OK, Mr. Arias, say this is you." The doctor motioned at the game board. "Normally, your neuro pathways conduct the electrical signals that your body sends to communicate like this." He demonstrated by inserting the game tweezers into the little organ cavity on the game board and let them touch the sides. The red nose lit up, and there was a loud buzzing sound. "See, his nose light up? The signals are normally sent without you having to be concerned about how they are being transmitted. It's a great game," the doctor said in a bit of nostalgia. "Have you ever played it?" Then he looked at Leigh and held the game out. "Here, do you want to try it?" There was no response from Juan.

Leigh chewed her gum. "No thanks, Doc. I don't want to play your little game. You don't still play with it, do you?"

The doctor smiled. "No, Mrs. Arias. I used to play it all the time as a boy. I was really good at it. We use it here as an instructional aid when speaking to children about certain medical conditions. Occasionally, Dr. Peabody and I have a match or two. He is not happy with me because I keep winning." The doctor caught himself from further rambling about his favorite childhood board game and turned back to Juan.

"When you were electrocuted, your body's neuro pathways were fried." He removed the battery from the game board. Then he inserted the tweezers into the same small organ cavity. Nothing happened.

"You see, just like the electrical pathways are turned off in this game, so your pathways have been turned off. When I say that you were fortunate, what I mean is that you would have most certainly died from the shock, but since these new pathways were available through your costume, which resulted from your ingesting the bonding agent, your body was able to continue to function and we were able to revive you. However, if we take the costume off, your body has no way of sending the signals that keep your body functioning. You would die in approximately three minutes."

Juan sank into the bed, in disbelief that this could be happening to him. "This is insane. It's not possible."

Leigh looked at Dr. Rashad, the official bearer of this bad news and said, "Great! Now, what are we supposed to do?"

The doctor did not answer. He spoke to them in a conciliatory tone. "I would not have thought this possible myself until today. Your condition is new to us, Mr. Arias. It's probably going to be awhile before we know how to treat you. Until then, you're perfectly fine as long as you remain in the rabbit suit. If you have to remove it, you must put it back on within three minutes. That's the time limit your body can sustain you without its ability to transmit signals throughout your body. I am sorry. I wish I had better news."

Juan repeated Leigh's question. "Doc, what am I supposed to do? This can't be happening to me."

Dr. Rashad looked at Leigh, then back at Juan. "I realize this is a lot to take in right now. We will explore every possible avenue until we find a way to treat you. Right now, you really should get some rest, Mr. Arias. We'll run a few more tests, then you will be free to go home and resume your normal life."

"Normal life?" Juan snapped. "Aren't you forgetting something, doc? I'm in a rabbit costume, for crying out loud! How am I supposed to resume a normal life? How will I bathe, or go to work? Holy cannoli!" Juan paused and looked at Leigh.

She knew what he was thinking. Leigh gave Juan a sarcastic glance. "Three minutes was more than enough time for you, hon, but you're not coming near me dressed like a rabbit."

The gravity of the situation hit Juan like a punch in the stomach. He cringed. "I cannot believe this is happening to me! What are the chances? Just what are the chances of something so weird happening to anybody on this planet? I've heard of people having all sorts of strange accidents, but this is ridiculous. Stuck in a rabbit costume? Give me a break!"

Juan was angry now, and he wanted to wake up from this nightmare. "Why me? I just don't get it. Why did I let myself be talked into dressing up like the Easter Bunny? What do rabbits have to do with Easter anyway? I don't think they're cute. Do you think they're cute, Leigh? I don't. They're fuzzy, so what? I just don't see what people get all happy about." Juan, now on the verge of hysteria, continued his rant, "Oh, look how cute with their little nose. Oh, look how cute their little tails are. Oh, look how they hop and frolic in the woods. Overgrown rodents make me wanna vomit. This whole Easter thing makes me sick. Why the hell do we celebrate Easter, anyway? What is the big deal? Jesus dies and comes back to life? Give me a break. You expect me to believe that, too? I must be an idiot. If there were a God, why would he let something like this happen to me? Is this how He gets his laughs?"

Dr. Rashad took Juan's hand. "Mr. Arias, please calm down." He held it for a moment. At once, Juan seemed to calm down. In fact, he seemed to go from being hysterical to calm in no time. Maybe it was Dr. Rashad's good bedside manner. Juan was quiet but seemed far away as the doctor spoke to him, "You will just have to plan your activities around your three-minute time limit. Aside from this, there is no reason why you can't function as you did before, as a perfectly normal human being. You may have to make special arrangements at work regarding dress code and get used to short showers. I'm sure you and your wife will work this out."

Leigh rolled her eyes again and looked up as she murmured to herself, "Why me?"

Dr. Rashad continued, "As far as Easter is concerned, I have no idea what a rabbit has to do with it. I'm not even sure what Easter is supposed to be about, aside from selling lots of candy and merchandise, that is. I'm not Christian, and I don't celebrate Easter, except for indulging in candy-coated almonds. I'm an atheist. You might say that science is my religion. Things like this are unfortunate accidents. There is no divine power playing a joke on you, Mr. Arias. Our lives are filled with random events. Sometimes strange things occur, but science can eventually figure things out. I have many friends who practice different religions, from Buddhists to Jews and everything in between. That is fine. People sometimes need to think there is something greater than them. It makes no sense, but if it makes people feel good, then that's fine. I prefer scientific fact, and I assure you there is a scientific solution to your problem. You just need to be patient and carry on with your life."

As Dr. Rashad finished his little ramble about science and religion, he noticed that Juan looked like he had an upset stomach. "Mr. Arias are you feeling sick? You don't look well all of a sudden."

Before he replied, Juan closed his eyes for a moment. "No, just a bit dizzy." Then he asked, "Doc, did you check my labs for Tularemia caused by the bacterium, Francisella tularensis?"

The doctor raised an eyebrow at the unexpected question. "Why, yes, Mr. Arias, I did! Do you have a medical background?"

"No," Juan replied.

"Then how do you know about all that medical stuff?" Juan seemed to be thinking the same thing as he looked at Dr. Rashad.

"I must have read something about it, I guess."

Dr. Rashad smiled. "You have a good memory. Maybe the electric shock triggered memories of things that you have read. This might be a good thing." He looked at Leigh and then at Juan. "After we run a few more tests, you are free to go home. It shouldn't take long."

The second nurse came into the room and asked the doctor if the other two people in the waiting room could come in and see the patient. Dr. Rashad turned to Juan and asked if it would be all right to admit the visitors. Juan gave him a quick nod. The nurse left the room and then Ray and Angie came in.

Angie was glad to see that Juan was alive and awake as she entered the room. "Thank God, you're all right!"

Ray was also glad to see his brother-in-law alive. "We all

feared the worst, Juan. I'm sorry this happened."

Juan sighed and tried to give a little smile but couldn't. "Yeah, me too. What's done is done."

"But you're going to be all right, right?" Ray noticed that Leigh and Juan did not look as though everything was fine. "What about the BD109 in his system? I thought it would have poisoned him. Geez, I'm so sorry about that, Juan. Wilma thought it was just another vial of food coloring after she knocked over my briefcase. When I saw that bright green residue in your glass as the paramedics were trying to revive you, I hoped it was just a new green food dye. I recognized that radioactive looking color, so I checked the vials on the table and found the empty BD109 vial. I thought you were going to die from poisoning. You used it as food coloring and ingested it with the lemonade."

Dr. Rashad raised his hand. "You can relax, Mr. Cromwell. The chemical your-brother-law ingested before he was electrocuted saved his life. I'm most certain of it."

Ray was amazed. "Really? How?"

"I'll let Juan explain what happened." Dr. Rashad handed the Operation board game to Juan. "I'd like to see you in a few days, Juan, to monitor how you are doing. The nurse will schedule the appointment. Well, goodnight all."

With that, Dr. Rashad left the room.

14

Post-Traumatic Rabbit Syndrome

They didn't say much on the way home. Each was preoccupied with their own thoughts. Juan and Leigh arrived at their house at 9:30 pm. Juan turned to Leigh. "Now what? I can't spend the rest of my life looking like this!"

Walking around dressed up like a rabbit on Easter Sunday was one thing. Doing it all year long was quite another.

Leigh was tired and didn't want to get into a discussion about it right then. The party was a bust, and now her husband had been sentenced to spending the rest of his life dressed like a rabbit. She couldn't be seen with him that way, and having any wine tasting parties at their house was out of the question until he could be rid of the dumb costume, but according to Dr. Rashad that might not be for a long time, if ever.

"I have a headache, Juan. I'm going to bed. Do you mind sleeping in the living room tonight? I just need a little time to get used to this."

"Sure, no problem. I'm just going to prepare a sandwich and watch a little TV before I hit the sack." He reached for her and took her hand. "We're going to get through this, right, Leigh? Maybe we'll wake up tomorrow morning, and it will turn out to be a bad dream."

Leigh gave him a half-hearted smile. "I hope you're right, Juan."

All of a sudden, Juan felt dizzy again, just like he had felt in the doctor's office. He sat on the sofa and closed his eyes for a moment.

Leigh noticed his change. "Are you all right?"

"Yeah, I'm just a little dizzy. I'll be OK."

"Good, I'm exhausted. I'm going to bed."

"Goodnight, Leigh."

As Leigh began to head to the bedroom, Juan asked, "Are you planning to visit a lawyer tomorrow?"

Leigh stopped dead in her tracks; she turned to look at Juan. "I just wanted to see if we could sue someone for what happened to you. The doctors don't have a clue how to cure you."

"Was that all, Leigh?"

She seemed nervous about the question. "Yeah."

"I don't think we have a case. It was an accident, and there were plenty of witnesses." Juan paused for a moment. "Why didn't you give back the extra money at the supermarket earlier today?"

Leigh froze. "What?"

He continued, "That cashier was pretty young. It might have been her first job, and she probably got into big trouble, maybe even got fired, for being short twenty dollars."

Leigh stood there feeling a little numb. "How do you know that, Juan? How can you possibly know that? Are you reading my mind? I never mentioned it to you." Leigh was beside herself. She felt violated in some strange way. "If the kid was stupid enough to give me an extra twenty, I wasn't going to be stupid enough to give it back."

After an uncomfortably long pause, Juan asked, "When were you going to tell me about your affair with Bill Fletcher?"

Leigh's mouth hung open. Her cheeks turned red. Then her eyebrows merged into a uni-brow with a double crease down the middle. She took a step toward Juan. "What?" She screamed as she stomped her foot. "Now you're accusing me of having an affair? I can't believe you!" Leigh roared, "You're stuck in that stupid rabbit costume for the rest of your life, and now you've turned into a mind-reading freak? I can't take this! I'm going to stay with Martha."

She raced into the bedroom and packed a suitcase. A few minutes later, the earth shook as Leigh stormed out of the house and slammed the door behind her.

Juan didn't bother making that sandwich after all. His appetite was gone. He sat on the couch looking at the television, which was not turned on. He just gazed at his reflection on the screen. Where a man should be sitting, there sat a giant rabbit.

15

The Discriminated Rabbit

The next morning, Juan got up at his usual time, to get ready for work. He went to the kitchen and grabbed the egg timer. He showered for exactly two and half minutes and spent twenty-seconds drying. He was back in the rabbit suit with a few seconds to spare.

He tried putting on a pair of pants and a shirt over the costume, but he could hardly move and he looked like the Michelin Man. After abandoning that idea, he cut a hole at the bottom of the rabbit feet so he could wear his normal shoes. He tried putting on his raincoat over the costume to conceal it as much as possible. He got hot quickly and had to keep it unbuttoned. Then he tied down the rabbit ears so that they laid flat on his head and ran down the back of his neck underneath his raincoat. Every time he tried that, however, he would get a pounding headache exactly three minutes later. He decided to let the ears be. *"This will have to do."*

After Ray and Angie had visited Juan at the hospital, they dropped off his car so that he would not have to arrange to pick it up the next day. As Juan got into his car, he took a deep breath, looked in the rearview mirror, shook his head and was off to work.

As soon as he was in traffic, the stares began. When he parked his car and started walking toward the office building, Detta Parson, a heavyset black woman who worked in the building, caught sight of him.

"Good morning, bunny man. Say, Easter's over, sugar. You

can take that off now."

Juan smiled. "Yeah, I know, but somebody triple-dog dared me." He continued to walk into the lobby and met more stares, smiles, and double takes as people watched what looked like an undercover bunny waiting for an elevator. He had to go to the seventh floor, so he stood waiting his turn to catch one of the four elevators.

"What's with the rabbit outfit?" Asked Joe Singleton, one of Juan's coworkers.

"It's a long story, Joe."

Finally, an elevator arrived. Juan got into it along with eight other people.

As the doors closed, Eduardo Rodriguez, one of the cleaning crew supervisors, commented in a heavy Latino accent. "Hey, Juan, is that the new dress code? Because if it is, I want no part of it, man!"

The people in the elevator tried to restrain from laughing, but one person trying hard not to laugh let out a snort. That set everybody else into uncontrollable laughter.

Juan turned almost as pink as his outfit. All he could think of saying was, "You people have no respect for the Easter Bunny."

The elevator doors opened. It was only the third floor. This was the longest elevator ride of Juan's life. Two people got off, still smiling. The doors closed again. No one said a word. A few people cleared their throats, trying not to laugh again. Juan felt like an hour had passed since he had stepped into the elevator. Next time, he would take the stairs. Juan watched the floors go by 4, 5, then it stopped at 6. Four more people got off.

One of the older women getting off turned to Juan and said, "Thanks for helping get my morning started with a good laugh. I really needed that. You have a blessed day."

The doors closed again. Finally, after what seemed like a week, the doors opened on the seventh floor. Juan and everyone except Eduardo got off.

"Hey, Juan." Juan turned to look at Eduardo, who held up two fingers. "Peace, bro." Juan smiled at Eduardo as the doors of the elevators closed.

Juan went straight to his desk and continued working on the software troubleshooting routine he had started on Friday. In the open bullpen seating arrangement, everybody could see the pair of rabbit ears sticking up. Everyone was curious, and coworkers came by and asked the same question: "What's with the rabbit outfit? Why are you dressed like that?"

He got very little done during the first part of the morning. At 11:35 his boss asked to see him. Mr. Preston's office was on the eighth floor, so Juan decided to take the stairs up one flight. As he entered the eighth floor offices, there were smiles and stares. He knocked on Mr. Preston's office door.

"Come in and close the door, Juan. Tell me why in the world you are dressed like that. All morning, all I've gotten are comments and giggle reports about how silly you look. Easter's over, man! What's this all about?"

Juan explained what had happened the day before. His boss listened intently as he recounted the bizarre series of events that had taken place.

Finally, Mr. Preston sat back in his chair. "Juan, you know I've always held you in the highest regard. You've been one of our most valued programmers. However, the situation as it is..." Mr. Preston paused for a moment. Juan dreaded what he thought might be coming out of his boss's mouth next. Then Mr. Preston continued. "I cannot have a giant rabbit running around our facility. I can't hide you every time a client comes by, and we have many of them coming through both seventh and eighth floors. I have to put you on a leave of absence until this rabbit condition is cleared up. You have one month of leave available to you. I suggest you take it. Go on vacation or something and we'll see how you are feeling after that time."

Juan pleaded, "Mr. Preston, you don't understand. I need to be busy. I think I'll go out of my mind if I'm not allowed to work. Can't I work from home?"

"You know our policy, Juan. All coding must be done on the premises. Due to the nature of our accounts and the multiple attempts we have had at hacking our system, this is the way it has to be. I cannot deviate from policy or protocol. I'm sorry."

Mr. Preston signaled to the two men now at his door. "Please, escort Mr. Arias directly to his vehicle. Do you understand?"

They both nodded. "Yes, sir."

Mr. Preston looked sincerely concerned. "Juan, I meant what I said. You are on leave. Please call me when you are better. I'd like to see you back here as soon as possible. You got that, Juan? I'll have your personal belongings delivered to your house."

Juan nodded, stood up and was escorted off the premises. Once in his car, he reached for his cell phone and called Leigh but got her voice mail. He did not leave a message.

His two escorts stood by and watched until he had started his vehicle and had driven off the company property.

It was just past noon. Juan decided to risk further ridicule. He stopped at his neighborhood supermarket for a few groceries. He picked up turkey cold cuts, some cranberry juice and several packs of marshmallow Peeps, which had been marked down. He hurried to the cashier as if trying to outrun all the looks and stares from the other shoppers.

As the cashier rang up his items, she glanced up at him and smiled. "Got a party to go to?"

Juan gave her a faint smile. "No, that was yesterday." He cast a blank stare at her. "This is the rest of my life." The faint smile disappeared. She gave him his change. He grabbed the bag and left the supermarket and tried calling Leigh again but got her voice mail.

As he exited the supermarket, a Boy Scout walked up to him. "Hello, sir, would you like to buy some..."

Juan did not want to stop for anybody. All he wanted was to get home, out of the staring crowd and talk to Leigh.

"Not now, kid." Juan sprinted past the boy and bumped the chocolate bars out of his hands. Juan didn't stop or bother to look back. He walked to his car, got in, and burned rubber out of the shopping center.

A rather large woman saw what happened and came over to the boy. "Are you hurt, young man?"

The boy was on his knees picking up the chocolate bars. "No, I don't think so."

The large woman huffed. "That nasty old rabbit knocked all of your things down. You sure you're OK, dear?"

"Yes, ma'am, I'm sure. Thank you."

The lady picked up one the chocolate bars and gently

brought it up to her nose. She closed her eyes and took a deep breath. "Say, are these chocolate bars with peanuts?"

The Boy Scout had recovered all of his fallen items. He turned to the woman. "Yes, ma'am. They're organic, fair-trade chocolate bars from one of the villages in South America, near the rainforest. This is the first time we are selling them. We're trying to support people in small villages, so they can make a living and don't have to cut down the rainforest."

"Well, aren't you sweet," the woman said as she pinched the boy's cheek affectionately. "I'll take one."

The boy handed her a bar. She looked up cheerfully. Her eyes were filled with delicious chocolate anticipation. "No, dear, I'll take one dozen."

Diogenes Ruiz

16

Ray Meets the Devil

Ray was not looking forward to his meeting with the new chairman. He knew that he needed to be careful. Peggy greeted him and buzzed Monty.

"Mr. Cromwell is here."

"I'll buzz you when I'm ready to see him." Monty replied.

Peggy told Ray to have a seat, that Mr. Monty McPride would be ready to see him shortly.

"I'm sorry to hear about Blake. How is he doing?"

She met his eyes. "Not very well, I'm afraid. There is no change in his condition. He is unable to speak or move for that matter. He needs constant monitoring."

"What exactly happened to him, Peggy?" Ray listened attentively as she relayed the facts of what had happened to Blake McPride. "Did he seem at all sick before his meeting with Monty?"

"No, he seemed fine. He had skipped taking his medicine before, but never experienced that kind of reaction. Although, I'm not sure how long he went without taking it."

Ray lowered his voice a bit and discreetly asked, "Was there anything that struck you as odd when you entered the room and saw what was happening?"

She thought for a moment. "No, Monty was leaning over his father crying. He was really upset. I was the one who called 911. Monty was too shaken up."

"I bet he was," Ray thought.

Peggy continued, "Then the paramedics and security arrived, and Blake was taken to the hospital. I guess the only thing that struck me as a little odd was when the security guard pointed to the doodle on Blake's desk and said that it was ironic that one moment you could be as happy as a lark and the next minute you could be on your way to the hospital. I just couldn't picture Blake doodling a happy face."

Then she paused and looked at Ray.

"Ray, do you think there was foul play in what happened to Blake?"

Ray took a deep breath. "I don't know, Peggy. The only thing I can say for sure is, don't let your coffee cup out of your sight if you happen to be drinking it when your boss is around."

She looked puzzled and was about to ask a question.

"Don't ask. I just know it would be a good idea."

At that moment, Monty buzzed Peggy, "Send him in."

"Yes, sir."

Ray went to Monty's office and gave a polite knock.

Monty did not look up right away. After a long moment he glanced at Ray. "Come in, Mr. Cromwell."

Ray entered the office not knowing quite what to expect from his new lunatic client.

"Sit." He did not bother to greet Ray. "As you know, Blake McPride has been taken ill."

Ray nodded. "Yes, I'm very sorry to hear..."

"Don't interrupt me, Mr. Cromwell," Monty reprimanded. "I am now in charge, and as I tried to enlighten you upon our first meeting, where you clumsily spilled Ms. Jones' coffee, Blake McPride's business is my business. I hope that is quite clear to you now." He paused and looked at Ray.

Ray simply nodded.

"I know that you and Blake had been working on the formula for the bonding agent. I need you to tell me where we are with the development. I understand that we are very far along, and there was just one more test before limited production could begin. Is that correct, Mr. Cromwell?"

"Yes, that is correct."

Monty remained silent, waiting for Ray to elaborate. Ray was not sure if the lunatic had finished speaking. He knew for sure that he needed to buy some time. He wasn't going to give Monty what he wanted, not just yet, not unless he absolutely had to. Fortunately, KC was the only other person who knew the outcome of the test.

Monty continued to stare at Ray. Then he flapped his arms as though he was conducting a symphony. "Well, Mr. Cromwell? Would you care to bring me up to date on the outcomes of the last test?"

Ray played dumb and completely cooperative. "Why, of course, Mr. McPride. I just wanted to make sure I didn't interrupt you. I wasn't sure if you had finished speaking."

Monty impatiently waved his hand. "Yes, yes, go on."

Ray gathered his thoughts then gave his progress report. "Our tests were going very well. Unfortunately, the last test had a few issues that are being analyzed. We hope to have a reformulated solution."

Monty frowned. "And what is the nature of these few issues, Mr. Cromwell?"

Ray thought quickly and responded with some technical jargon regarding the test parameters and then summarized: "The bonding failed to reach a critical threshold. Basically, the cellular bonding adhesion failed."

Monty was annoyed hearing this. "And when will you have this corrected, Mr. Cromwell?"

Ray thoughtfully considered the question and figured that six months would be reasonable. "We've already started to work on the problem, Mr. McPride, and we anticipate having the problem resolved in six months."

Monty rose from his chair, "You have one week."

Ray fell silent and started to say, "But that is imposs..."

"You have one week, Mr. Cromwell, and I want a finished working bonding agent, just as the progress reports you submitted to my idiot father indicated that you had almost completed. If you cannot deliver the completed formulation on spec as I was led to believe, I will bring in Delta Labs to finish our product. As per our contract, you will provide them all the test materials and project notes that have been part of this study to date. Is that understood, Mr. Cromwell?"

"Yes, I understand."

"Good day, Mr. Cromwell. That will be all. I expect you here next week at the same time for your final report."

Ray got up and started to leave.

Monty cleared his throat, signaling that he was not through speaking after all. "Oh, Mr. Cromwell, I don't know what you suspect may have happened to my father, but I can assure you that no one is more upset to see him in this condition than I. You see, it was I who saved his life. If he had been alone when his symptoms began, he would have surely died."

Ray turned and tried not to let Monty see his shock and disbelief at that statement. *"You lying murderer, you won't get away with it.*

The acting chairman continued, "And I don't know why you think people should guard their coffee when I'm around. Perhaps you think you saw something which you did not actually see. No matter, Mr. Cromwell, your business will be done here soon enough. And please remember, I know everything that is going on at my company."

It was now obvious that Monty had been eavesdropping on his conversation with Peggy. Were the telephones tapped as well? Ray was now convinced that whatever had happened to Blake McPride was no accident. How he was going to prove it, he had no idea.

Monty summoned Fred Wilkins after Ray left the office.

"Come in and shut the door. Is the remote lab ready?"

Fred smiled, "We're all set. Do we have a product that we can begin to produce?"

Monty was still irritated. "No, not yet, but we will have it next week whether it's ready for its intended medical purpose or not. We will begin replicating our little super drug nevertheless. I don't give a rat's ass if it helps burn victims as long as it lives up to its addiction potential."

Ray's mind was spinning. He called KC and told him not to take any calls until he arrived and they had a chance to talk. He headed straight for the testing lab. Ray's bad feeling about Monty was confirmed today by everything he had heard.

As Ray entered the lab area and walked toward KC's office, he motioned to KC. KC came through the lab and met Ray in the office.

"What's going on, Ray?"

"Remember what I asked you about BD109 data?"

KC could see that Ray was stressed about something. "Yeah, not to release the findings yet, right?"

"That's right, and if Monty McPride personally calls, do not give him any additional information. Got that? You also need to make sure that we are not compromised by anyone on staff. We can't afford to inadvertently release the data. It's very important, KC. I think Monty McPride is insane or crazy. You pick one. I can't prove it yet, but there must be a way. He's given me a week to give him the working formula for BD109. If I do not, he will pull the project and give it to Delta Labs. So, at best, we have a week to keep the data to ourselves."

"Don't worry, Ray. I'll tidy up a bit, so the data is only accessible through my personal handheld, which I keep in the bottom drawer of my desk." KC went over and pulled out the small device and held it up. "It's my practice box for gaming competitions. User name Superfly, with a capital S, password 4moelarry&curly. Best to remember it; don't write it down."

In spite of the seriousness of the subject at hand, Ray just had to ask, "Superfly? 4MoeLarry&Curly? What are you a sci-fi nut and bad comedy nerd?"

KC figured Ray must have had a deprived childhood. "C'mon, Ray, don't tell me you've never heard of *Superfly*, one of the early and best black exploitation movies of all time? We were just coming into our own on the big screen. He was 'The Man' back in that era. He was the black James Bond. And how could you not love the Stooges, three of the most stupid white guys you'd ever seen? Ray, mi amigo, you need to expand your appreciation of black culture. You do know who Duke Ellington is, right? I mean, you are not completely void of appreciating great entertainment, I hope? I'll have to take you under my wing and learn you some good movies, son."

Ray chuckled. "And you're in charge of the lab? God help us."

KC put his handheld back in the drawer.

"Hey, KC, all kidding aside, this is serious. Monty is nuts, and I don't think he likes black people or anybody who is not white. I saw him spit into one of the administrator's coffee cup, when she wasn't looking. He talked to the Latino janitor like he was talking to a dog, and he referred to his father who is lying in the hospital as 'my idiot father.' No love lost there."

"What are you going to do, Ray? A week's not a whole lot of time, and there's no way the lab won't comply with whatever Monty wants to do. We signed a contract, and this is legally their project."

Ray knew that KC was right. Unfortunately, he didn't have any proof, or a plan for that matter.

"I don't know what I'm going to do, KC, but I do know that having a week is better than nothing."

17

Rabbits Need Not Apply

"How are you feeling Juan? Has there been any change in your condition?" Angie had him on speaker phone as she prepared dinner. It was almost time for Ray to be getting home.

"Physically, I'm OK, but being stuck in this rabbit outfit is miserable. I'm the laughing stock everywhere I go. Leigh and I had a big fight last night. She walked out. She is staying at Martha's but won't take my calls. I got fired. Technically, I was put on leave of absence. I guess then they can fire me. Other than that, it was a peachy day."

Angie paused as she heard about Juan's rotten day. "Oh, I'm sorry, Juan. I'm sure things will work themselves out. Leigh probably just needs a little time to adjust, and you will probably be able to return to work before thirty days. Just try to stay positive. Why don't you come over and have dinner with us tonight?"

Juan was not up to going anywhere tonight. He hoped that Leigh would come home. "Thanks, Angie, but I think I'll stay here tonight, just in case Leigh comes home. I'm sorry that I ruined the kids' Easter party. I hope none of the kids got permanent brain damage after seeing the Easter Bunny get fried."

Angie reassured him. "The kids are OK. They were concerned that you had died, but they were relieved when we told them that the Easter Bunny got a nasty shock but was still alive. Wilma was the one who was shaken up, but she is OK now. You can come by tomorrow if you'd like and spend some time."

Juan had other plans for the day. "I spent the afternoon scanning for jobs. I called up a few and wound up getting an interview. It's with a software startup, and I need to be there in the morning."

Angie was relieved that he was reporting something positive. "That's great, Juan. I hope you get it." She heard Matthew and David greet their father as he came into the house. "Juan, good luck tomorrow. I gotta run. Ray just came home, and I'm getting dinner ready. Let me know how it goes."

"Will do. Love you, sis. Say hi to Ray, and thanks for bringing my car over yesterday."

"OK, Juan. Love you, too. Bye."

Juan hung up and tried Leigh's phone. This time he left her a message. "Leigh, it's Juan. Please call me. Let's talk."

Juan entered the lobby of the software company's building. He wore his long raincoat and did his best to appear normal. He received a few double takes and smiles but did not engage anyone in rabbit conversation. He went over to the directory and found what he was looking for, Blakk Boxx Software, Suite 119. *"Thank goodness it's on the first floor."*

He arrived at Suite 119 and entered slowly. It was a creative-looking place. It was a young company. Their first game release had been a huge success. There were product posters and displays decorating the small waiting area. Juan approached the receptionist's desk. There was nobody there. He could hear someone in the adjacent room which appeared be the copy room.

The receptionist came out of the room and stood behind the counter. She gave Juan a look over. "Look mister, I'm not sure what you're selling, but I ain't interested. There's a no soliciting sign." She pointed to the door.

"I'm actually here for the interview with Mr. Smith for the programming job."

The receptionist now had a smirk on her face. "You're kidding, right?"

Juan ignored the smirk as well as her oddly pierced nose, chin, snake tattoo on her neck, multiple pierced ears with plugs in her ear lobes. "Do I look like I'm kidding?"

She made a motion with her hand like Vanna White

demonstrating a product. "You're dressed like a giant rabbit. You've got to be kidding."

He thought to himself, *"And you look like a slice of badly dressed Swiss cheese,"* but did not say anything. For all he knew, he might be working here soon and didn't want to get off on the wrong foot with anybody in the office.

Juan wondered, *"How could she possible think I look odd by comparison?"* He had a rabbit costume on, and she was wearing a picture of a snake and a pound of silver, all of it above the neck and had gaping holes in her ears. "I spoke with Mr. Smith about the position yesterday. He is expecting me."

She gave him an OK-but-you'll-be-sorry look. "OK, but the job is for a programmer, not a rabbit. Don't lay an egg if he doesn't hire you."

"Can you just let him know I'm here, please? I don't want him to think that I arrived late for my interview."

The young woman pressed the intercom. "Mr. Smith, this is the front desk. There's a large, nasty rabbit out here."

Mr. Smith came on the line. "Well, call someone in maintenance and have it removed." She giggled silently and put a hand over her mouth. "Actually, Juan Arias is here to see you."

"OK, good, I'll be done here in ten minutes. Please show him to my office then."

When she was off the intercom, she motioned to Juan, "Have a seat. I'll take you to his office in just a few. He's way on the other side."

Juan took a seat and waited eagerly.

A few employees walked by on their way out of the office. One of them stopped to look at Rabbit Man. "Bunny gram? Who's getting the bunny gram?"

Juan smiled and replied, "Mr. Smith."

The worker's smile widened. "Oh man, I wish it were for me!" Then the group continued out the door.

"I'd offer you some carrots, but we're all out," the receptionist said as she smirked. Then the intercom crackled, and Mr. Smith came back on. "Medusa, show Mr. Arias in. I'm ready."

Juan's ears perked up. She stood up, and he stood up, ready to go to Mr. Smith's office. "Medusa? Your name is Medusa?" Juan was unable to conceal his smile.

She looked at him and popped her gum. "Yeah, cool huh? OK, now, I'm going to take you to Mr. Smith's office, so you have to walk this way." She then proceeded to hop down the corridor. She didn't look back. She just kept hopping.

They passed a coworker, and he remarked, "New boyfriend, Medusa?"

She ignored him and kept hopping. Finally, she came to a stop in front of Mr. Smith's office.

"OK, Mr. Bunny, hop right in," she said and turned to go back to her post.

Juan entered the office and saw Mr. Smith poking his head into his file cabinet. He talked while he fished for a file.

"Have a seat. Tell me about yourself. What experience do you have with diagnostic programming?" Finally, he found his file, spun in his chair and caught sight of Juan. "What's with the costume?"

Juan didn't want to blow this interview. He needed to keep the focus on his programming skills, so he decided to keep his explanation brief. "It's a special condition that I have. I have to wear it, or I'll die."

Mr. Smith nodded as though he understood. "Do you feel this way about costume wear in general or just this particular outfit?"

Juan quickly responded, "No, my personal feelings have nothing to do with it. I just have to wear this rabbit costume, or I'll die, really! It's a medical condition."

"I see. Did you always have these feelings and tendencies or did they develop as you were growing up?"

"Actually, I had an accident. It happened quite by accident."

"When did this accident occur?"

"It happened while I was entertaining kids on Easter Sunday, but it has not affected my programming skills. I'm quite good and have good references."

"I don't doubt what you say, Mr. Arias. Unfortunately, there is no way I can hire you if you have to dress like that every day. I have to admit, in one respect you would fit right in. God knows I have enough freaks running around this place. We are a freaky software company, you might say, but a giant rabbit would hurt our freak image. We cater to an urban, gritty gaming audience. I'm afraid you'd be spreading too much sunshine in the rabbit costume. It's all about attitude, Mr. Arias. Mean, dirty, punkish, in-your-face imagery. That's what helps us sell product. If word got out that Blakk Boxx Software hired the Easter Bunny, we'd be screwed."

Juan spent the next couple of days calling and visiting employment agencies. Most laughed him out without any serious consideration. He tried repeatedly to get in touch with Leigh, but she still would not return his calls.

18

Having a Bad Day?

It was late morning on Wednesday, and Juan had just visited another employment agency. He was tired of the stares, the stupid remarks, and the well-meaning smiles from people who hadn't the slightest clue of what it was like for him to be trapped in a cartoon character's artificial skin. He was a minority of one. His stomach began to grumble. He'd been craving his favorite barbecue sandwich. As much as he dreaded the thought of going to a crowded mall for a sandwich, his stomach won out, and he headed for Smitty's.

Juan arrived at the mall and headed straight for the food court. As he entered, his nose was seduced by the delicious scents from the various food vendors. His mouth began to water He ignored the stares and stood in line.

It was always busy at the mall at lunch time, especially at Smitty's. After five minutes in line, a young man took his order. Juan ordered his usual, a pulled barbecue pork sandwich with a side of coleslaw, a cola, and a piece of apple pie. It had been a while since Juan visited his favorite eatery.

"Thank you, nineteen cents is your change." The counter boy handed Juan his change. "What's with the costume, dude?" Everybody behind the counter paused to look at Juan. They all wondered the same thing.

Juan glanced at them. "I work for a costume manufacturer, and they have us wear these for publicity. You probably see it all the time, especially here at the mall."

"Oh yeah, cool." Everybody behind the counter went back to work.

In another couple of minutes Juan had his tray with the mouth watering sandwich, neatly sliced down the middle into two perfect halves for easy eating. He walked to a table and sat down to partake of his feast.

He had gotten to the food court just in time. It was quickly filling up with shoppers and with people who worked in the area. Juan sat down, but could not begin to dive into his feast because he had forgotten to pick up napkins. He usually grabbed a handful. Smitty's sandwiches were so juicy that you inevitably made a mess.

As he made his way to the side of the counter, Juan felt like a ton of bricks dropped on him when he saw Leigh sitting on the other side, at the Chinese food pavilion with Bill Fletcher. What should he do? He didn't want to make a scene at the mall, but he sure would like to get his hands on Bill Fletcher. Were they still having an affair? Juan's head started spinning. He paused looking at them, making sure that they were not seeing him.

After watching them for a few minutes, he decided not to confront her just yet. He would think before he did or said anything. Maybe while he ate he would have a better idea what to do. It looked like they had just sat down. Their plates were full.

Juan made his way back to his table and was amazed at another sight.

"People have some nerve! You can't even leave your food alone for a minute in a crowded mall because someone will take it!" Not only did someone steal his food, the guy had the nerve to be eating it right there. *"Didn't he think the owner of the food tray would come back and catch him? What gall."* He headed over to confront the food thief, a middle-aged black man. *"He probably does this regularly."* He looked very familiar though. *"I know I've seen him before, maybe right here. Who knows how many people he has stolen from and gotten away with it. Well, he's not getting away with stealing my lunch,"* Juan sat down directly across from the food thief. He waited for the guy to look up at him. The food perpetrator had evidently just started on Juan's lunch. He had half of Juan's sandwich in his hand and had taken one or two bites. He

had not yet started on the other half.

The food thief sensed that Juan was staring at him, but did not look up right away. Juan was determined not to be ignored. So he reached over and picked up the other half of the sandwich and took a big bite. He could feel his ears get angry hot. Juan chomped on the half sandwich without taking his eyes off the perpetrator, who slowly looked up. *"Yeah, you better be scared, buddy."*

The food thief looked up and their eyes locked. Juan kept chewing on his half of the sandwich waiting to hear what kind of lame excuse the thief would try to hustle. As they stared at each other for a moment, the food thief glanced at the side of Juan's mouth, which was now dripping with barbecue sauce. Then he picked up a napkin from the pile and handed it to Juan.

Without even realizing that he did so, Juan took the napkin and wiped his face. *"This guy is really slick. He gives me MY napkin to wipe MY mouth as he eats the other half of MY sandwich. What is this guy, insane? Does he think we're pals because he gave me MY napkin?"* Juan was determined to make this guy come clean. Thus far, neither black man nor pink rabbit had spoken a word. The food thief finished his half of Juan's sandwich and Juan was still eating the last bit of his. The whole time he had not taken his eyes off the bum. Juan's thought was, *"There is no such thing as a free lunch, buddy, and if you think I am going to let you get away with this, you're in for a big surprise."* Juan was going to call the security guard and have this guy arrested or at least made to pay for what he had stolen. With each bite, Juan got hotter under the collar. His original preoccupation with seeing Leigh and Bill Fletcher had been pre-empted by the lunch-stealing perpetrator.

Juan was now completely amazed at the nerve of this bum. The guy cut the piece of apple pie into two pieces and slid a piece over to Juan. *"That son of a cracker smacker, he's playing with me now. He's taunting me with my own dessert, and look at how he kept the fork!"* The bum ate his half of Juan's apple pie, and Juan just watched him. Finally, when the food thief was finished, Juan gave him a piercing look, grabbed the remaining half piece of pie and shoved it into his mouth, making loud savoring sounds. He let the pie pieces drip and flake against his mouth and made rude-sounding groans at the food thief.

After he devoured the half piece of pie, he simply stared at the bum sitting across from him. Then the food thief did it again. He handed Juan a napkin. This time Juan grabbed it out his hands, quickly wiped his mouth and shot up out of his chair to call the security guard.

He spotted one not too far on the other side of the court. He waved his arms and headed for the security guard. "Hey, security! I need your help over here." He walked toward the guard then he froze in his rabbit tracks as he spotted a food tray sitting on a table. He approached it to get a closer look. "This couldn't be mine," Juan mumbled. "That crazy black guy stole my lunch. I'm sure of it…I think." He got right up close and examined the contents of the tray: one uneaten barbecue sandwich neatly sliced in half, a side of coleslaw, a cola, and a piece of apple pie. The change was still on the tray. There was one dime, one nickel and four pennies.

Juan started to turn to look back at the man whom he thought had eaten his lunch, but the mall security guard arrived.

"What is it buddy? You need help over here?"

Juan turned to the security guard. "Uhh, no, I'm sorry. I thought something had been stolen, my lunch tray. Everything's fine. Sorry to bother you."

The guard looked at Juan's tray. "Barbecue pork, aye? What, you tired of carrots?" With that, the guard walked away.

Juan picked up the tray and headed for the table where he helped himself to the nice stranger's lunch, to apologize. Too late, the man was gone. Then he thought of Leigh. Would she still be there with Bill Fletcher? Juan made his way to the side of Smitty's counter to peek across the food court. They were gone.

Juan stood next to the line of people at Smitty's. "Anybody want a sandwich? I haven't touched it, got it about fifteen minutes ago, lost my appetite." Nobody said anything.

Juan grabbed his nineteen cents and took the tray. He came upon a young man trying to decide which food vendor to visit. "Here you go sir, compliments of Smitty's."

The fellow was pleasantly surprised. He gave Rabbit Man a big smile. "Hey, thanks man!"

Juan kept moving and left the mall. He headed to his car thinking about the complete stranger who sat patiently while he made an ass of himself eating the nice man's food. He replayed every bit of his lunch over in his mind and wondered why the stranger let him do it. *"Was he afraid of me?"* Juan wondered, and then thought that a guy in a rabbit costume was probably not too threatening. Yet he had that distinct feeling that he knew the man from somewhere.

Juan's mind was wandering. Thinking about Leigh and Bill Fletcher one moment and then about the polite stranger at the mall the next. As he pulled out of the shopping center, he almost hit another vehicle. With his mind preoccupied, he over swung the turn. A moment later, he saw the flashing blue light in his rearview mirror.

Juan pulled over and sat in his car mumbling profanities to himself under his breath. He hadn't gotten a ticket in over fifteen years, and now he was about to get his second in less than a week. He pulled the rabbit ears back so they were flat against his back. He knew he would get a headache if this took more than three minutes, but he didn't want the cop to think he was some kind of crazy.

He sat there looking ahead watching the traffic up at the next block as some idiot ran the red light and almost caused a major accident. He hoped that the cop would take off after that guy and forget about him. No such luck. The trooper's door opened, and officer Lockjaw stepped out.

Juan's mouth slowly sagged open. It was the same cop who stopped him on Easter. *"What was it with this guy? Does he have it out for me?"* Mumbled profanities flowed from the irritated rabbit's mouth as the trooper came up to the driver's side door. Juan lowered his window. Officer Lockjaw, whose real name was Michael Brubeck, looked into the vehicle.

"Well, Mr. Bunny man, license, please."

Juan handed him his license. *"It hasn't changed since the last time you looked at it, you tobacco chewing ignoramus."*

Officer Lockjaw was still chewing something. Juan wondered if the guy ever gave his jaw a rest. After so much working out he could probably chew through brick.

Bunny man remained silent. As the officer wrote the ticket, he couldn't help notice the shiny little object that was pinned to officer Lockjaw's shirt. It was small but had a brilliant gold shine as it reflected the sun. Juan made it out. It was a small cross. As the officer finished writing the ticket, Juan pointed to it. "Is that cross on your shirt law enforcement department-issued?"

Officer Brubeck handed the driving citation to him. "No, sir. It was issued by a much higher authority." He walked back to his cruiser, climbed back in, and took off. Juan put the ticket in the glove compartment on top of his previous citation. *"Only a couple of streets away, what rotten luck to get a ticket so close to home."*

He pulled up to his house. As he stepped into his small foyer, he glanced toward the kitchen and noticed a note stuck to the refrigerator. He pulled off the little wine bottle magnet, removed the note, and sat down at the kitchen table to read Leigh's letter.

Dear Juan,

I met with the lawyer on Monday and asked him to draw up divorce papers. I'm sure you won't object after learning of my affair with Bill Fletcher. I'm not sure how you found out, but I guess it's for the best. I don't think you and I are a good match any more. There is no sense going on pretending, especially after your accident. I just can't live with someone who has to be in a rabbit costume the rest of his life.

I'm sorry if I hurt you. Take care of yourself.

Leigh

Juan sat motionless for a moment. Then he got up and went to the bedroom and found all of Leigh's belongings and clothes gone. He went back to the kitchen, sat down at the table again, picked up the note and gazed at it for a while. He let it fall from his hand. Then he stood up, unzipped the rabbit suit, took it off and put it on the kitchen table. He stood in his underwear at the kitchen's entrance looking at the picture taken of him and Leigh, just before they were married. Three minutes later, he collapsed onto the floor.

19

Necessary Alliance

Ray needed to speak with Peggy Simmons in private, but dared not call her at work or go to McPride Industries since he did not know what areas might be safe to speak in private. He also did not dare send her an email, since it was probably being monitored. He did not have her personal email address. To contact Peggy and not raise suspicion, Ray hired a courier service to deliver a get well card for Blake McPride to Monty's office. He knew it would have to go to Peggy first. He instructed the courier to deliver the card to Peggy, along with a small note that was only to be delivered to Peggy and no one else. The envelope was labeled Monty McPride, in neat writing. The other was a hand-scribbled note. Ray paid extra to have them execute his instructions exactly at 11:45 am. Ray waited at the coffee shop up the street.

At precisely 11:45 am, the courier entered the building and checked in, telling security that he had a special delivery for Monty McPride to be left with Ms. Peggy Simmons, Mr. McPride's personal secretary. He was admitted and immediately made his way to Ms. Simmons' desk.

Peggy was at her desk and Monty was also there, handing her some papers. The courier had been instructed not to deliver the personal note to Peggy unless she was alone.

The courier approached the desk. Monty and Peggy both looked up at him. "I have a delivery for Ms. Peggy Simmons."

Monty ignored him and kept talking to Peggy. "I need a

new background check run on the board members. I am most interested in the ones that were particularly close to Blake, and I need the rest of the files, any hard copy memos which might not have been in my old man's office regarding BD109." Then he walked into his office without paying any further attention to the courier.

"Yes, sir," Peggy replied as Monty walked away.

Then she turned to the courier. "So you have a delivery?"

"Yes, ma'am. It's for Mr. Monty McPride. Just sign here, please." She signed the receipt. "Thank you, Ms Simmons."

She smiled back. Then the courier touched his lips, making the universal shush sign, and quickly handed her Ray's note. He turned and left before she could ask him anything.

Peggy quickly glanced at the note, which read:

Peggy,

Your desk is bugged. We need to meet right away. It's very important. Please do not let Monty know. Destroy this note after you read it. I'll be waiting at Cup-a-Hoot down the street – will explain when I see you.

- A friend

It was lunchtime, so this was as good a time as any to see what this was all about. She forwarded her calls to Alice, who typically took lunch at 1:00 pm. Then she headed down to the coffee shop.

Ray hoped that everything went smoothly with the delivery of the note as he waited at one of the tables toward the back. Upon seeing Peggy enter, he waved to her. She spotted him and seemed relieved that at least it was somebody she recognized.

"I was wondering who sent me that note." She sat down at his table.

"Thanks for meeting with me, Peggy. I wasn't sure you would come, but I had to risk it."

"What's this all about, Ray? My desk is bugged? Are you sure? Why?"

"I know this may sound crazy, but I don't think that what

happened to Blake McPride was an accident. I think Monty had something to do with it. When I met with him this past Monday, he spoke of things that you and I had talked about when I was waiting to see him. There is no other way he could have known of those things without overhearing our conversation. He wanted to know why I asked you to guard your coffee when he was around. The only other person I asked to guard her coffee was Latisha Jones after I saw Monty spit into her cup. He was quite sure that no one saw him, but I did as I was coming out of the restroom. Earlier that morning, I had a progress report meeting with Blake regarding BD109. I thought I might have imagined the spit fest. I've never seen a person do something like that before. Monty creeps me out, and I know he is up to something."

Peggy looked surprised but not shocked. "Do you think he did something to Mr. Blake intentionally so that he could be in charge?"

"Yes, but I also think he's got something in the works for BD109. He gave me exactly one week to get the formulation corrected. If I don't deliver, he will hire Delta Labs to take over the project. I'm not sure what is going on, Peggy, but I tell you Monty McPride is one sick individual. I also think he's quite dangerous. You need to watch yourself and your coffee."

Peggy looked at Ray and cringed at the thought of Monty's actions. "Why would a grown man do something so disgusting?"

Ray remembered Monty's behavior with the Spanish janitor. "From what I can tell, he doesn't much care for anybody who is not white." Ray then asked her something that had been troubling him ever since he got her voicemail message. "Peggy, how on earth did the board of directors let this lunatic take over?"

"The board was powerless to do anything. Blake McPride was considering retirement and the board knew it. They knew that he had a weak spot for Monty. If any other employee had performed as poorly as Monty, he would have been fired long ago. Some board members feel that Blake caved in and promoted his son, against his better judgment. When Monty presented them with the signed authorization, designating him as the new CEO, they were forced to comply. I'm not sure if anybody seriously suspects Monty had anything to do with his father being in the hospital. I am the recording secretary at the board meetings, and I can tell you that there is a great deal of concern among the board, but they are powerless to go against Mr. Blake McPride's wishes. I wish John Delmont was here. He would figure out a way to have Monty ousted." Then she paused. A light bulb went off in her head.

Ray finished the thought for her. "Surely, there must be something to incriminate him if he is responsible."

"What do you want me to do, Ray?"

"For now, let's exchange cell phone numbers. If anything should come up, I will contact you. I don't have a plan, and going to the police won't help us without the proper evidence. I do know that, come Monday, Monty will probably fire our firm, if only to get rid of me. He suspects that I know something and he is used to getting his way." Ray paused and gave a quick glance around to make sure no one was eavesdropping. "Just be on your toes, Peggy. Keep your eyes open for anything that might help us get to the bottom of this."

"I've noticed that he meets with Fred Wilkins quite often. He is the head computer geek. For the past few days, they've met just about every day, sometimes twice a day. Fred is Monty's right hand man now."

There have also been several meetings with men who claim to be friends of Monty. They don't strike me as the type that we would have as clients. They look more like pimps than corporate executives. It was not like that before Blake went to the hospital. I've also noticed that Monty has started referring to his father as 'the old man.' Before, he would refer to him as 'the chairman.' He is also getting ruder by the day."

"See if you can find out why Fred and Monty are meeting, but be careful. If he suspects anything, you'll be out of a job or possibly worse. By the way, Peggy, is there any change in Blake's condition?"

"No, I'm afraid not. They're moving him out of the hospital and into a round-the-clock care facility this weekend. The hospital called me and asked me to inform Monty."

"I'm sorry to hear that."

"Yes, me too, Blake was a good boss."

Ray nodded and looked at his watch. "I need to get going. Peggy, I don't want to take up your entire lunch hour. Thanks for meeting with me and don't forget, be careful."

20

Scout's Honor

Today was the last day to meet his goal. Ten year old Ben Gonzalez was combing the neighborhood selling chocolate bars. His orders did not have to be in until the next day, at his after-school Scout meeting. Fortunately, school let out early today. He was only six bars short of his goal. He hoped to sell that many and possibly a few more this afternoon, going door to door at the apartment complex located near his home. Ben's mom waited in the car and kept an eye on him as he knocked on doors.

The apartment complex was a strategic place to sell because he could cover multiple households in one location. Ben knocked on a few doors and sold two more bars. Many people were still at work, but he figured there were also some who stayed home. He would knock on the door, even if he thought no one was home. Sometime it was hard to tell.

Ben stood in front of the next door. As he prepared to knock, he heard a loud thud. He hesitated for a moment. All was quiet again. He knocked, and the door moved ever so slightly. He knocked again, and it opened wide enough that he could see inside the apartment. Ben gasped when he saw the man lying on the floor, dressed only in his underwear.

In true Boy Scout fashion, he rushed to the man's side. *"That must have been the thud I heard"* He dialed 911 and then signaled to his mom to come in. He looked at the building number on the outside of the apartment and gave the 911 operator the name of the apartment complex, which he remembered from the sign as they drove in.

"Do you know CPR?" asked the 911 operator.

"Yes," Ben replied.

"OK, son, keep him warm and I'll guide you through what to do." Ben glanced around for something to keep the man warm. He grabbed what looked like a fuzzy pink blanket and threw it over the man. *"It's not a blanket, but this should do the trick."* He quickly got down on his knees, felt for a pulse and followed the instructions given by the 911 operator.

Ben's mother walked in and saw her son applying CPR to the stranger. She did not interrupt him. He had set his cell phone on speaker phone. It was next to him as he continued to follow the 911 operator's instructions. A few minutes later he heard the sound of a siren approaching. The ambulance rolled up shortly thereafter. As the paramedics came into the apartment, Ben stood up and got out of the way. Juan was rushed to the hospital.

The suicidal rabbit woke up and saw Dr. Rashad standing over him.

Dr. Rashad had a frown on his face. "That was a dumb thing you did, Juan. I told you that removing the costume for more than three minutes would kill you. You are lucky to be alive, thanks to this good fellow who found you when he knocked on your door."

Juan glanced over at the Boy Scout. It was the same one he bumped into as he was leaving the supermarket.

"You again?" He rolled his eyes. "You are determined to sell me cookies, aren't you?"

"Actually, they're chocolate bars," Ben replied. "It's for our church's fundraiser."

"He found you passed out on the floor and covered you with the rabbit suit to keep you warm until the paramedics arrived. That saved your life."

Juan looked over at the Boy Scout. "I hope you don't think this means that I have to buy any of your chocolate bars."

"No," he politely replied. "I just wanted to make sure you were OK."

Juan looked over at the woman sitting next to the Boy

Scout. "And who's that?"

"That's my mom."

Ben's mother stepped forward. "I'm glad you're all right."

Juan looked at her. "I'm far from all right, but I suppose I should thank you for raising such a good kid." He glanced at Ben. "And I should thank you for saving my life."

"You're welcome," Ben replied.

Ben's mother put her arm around her son's shoulder. "I think we'd better get going."

As they started to leave, Juan asked, "Hey, kid, what's your name?"

"Ben," he replied.

Juan signaled to the boy to come closer. "Oh well, thank you, Ben. I'm Juan." He shook Ben's hand. "I'll take twelve of those chocolate bars."

"You really don't have to do that," Ben's mother replied.

Juan held up his hand. "No, no, I want to." Then he looked at Ben. "And, what is your mom's name?"

The Scout replied, "Linda. That's my mom's name."

Juan looked at them. "Well, I'm grateful to you both."

He extended his hand and shook Linda's hand. All at once, he felt dizzy and closed his eyes for a bit. Dr. Rashad noticed Juan's sudden disorientation. "What's the matter, Juan, are you still getting those dizzy spells?"

Juan opened his eyes. "Yeah, every once in a while it just hits me. It doesn't last long, then, I'm all right."

Juan looked at Ben. "What information do you need, and can I pay you when I get them? It seems I left my wallet at home."

Ben looked at Linda. She gave him a quick nod.

"OK," Ben replied. "I just need to get your information filled out on this form. We'll deliver your chocolate bars on Friday. That's when they come in."

Juan sat in his living room surrounded by his junk food mess, watching the news. *"What is wrong with the world? How can there be so much killing and random violence?"* He turned off the television and heard a knock at the door.

He glanced at the mess in the living room and dashed to

pick up the Cheetos and soda cans that he'd left lying around. In his mad dash to clean up, he tripped and fell. He got up again and continued his cleaning frenzy.

"Are you all right in there?" came a voice from the door. Linda and Ben looked at each other.

Juan finally opened the door. "Yeah, I'm fine. Come in."

"We've got your twelve chocolate bars," Ben announced as they entered. "I just need you to sign here."

"Great, thanks." Juan signed the delivery form. "Whoops, let me get the money to pay you." He dashed into the other room.

Linda could not contain her curiosity. "I know it's none of my business, but how did you get stuck wearing that outfit? The doctor said you could not survive without it."

Juan came in from the other room with cash in hand. "It's a long story. I had a freak accident while entertaining my sister's kids at an Easter party. Somehow, this was the result. My body's electrical signals are transmitted through the fabric in the costume now, so I need to keep it on or else."

"Oh my, that's awful."

"I can only be out of it for three minutes. After that, lights out."

She was curious. "Why were you out of it when Ben found you?"

Juan looked down, feeling embarrassed. "It just got to be too much, I guess. I've turned into a medical marvel or freak as some call it. My wife has filed for divorce. I've lost my job, gotten two traffic tickets, by the same cop no less, and managed to make a fool of myself at the mall, when I mistakenly accused a nice man of stealing my food tray. And to top it off, I've been rejected by every employment agency in the city. I guess it just got to be too much. If I had work, it wouldn't be so bad."

"Did you take those?" Linda pointed at the photographs hanging on the wall.

"Yeah, it was a hobby of mine. I haven't done much of it in a while."

"They're beautiful." She paused to look at some of the other photos on the wall. "Well, I hope things improve for you." Then she turned to her son. "Come on, Ben, let's get going."

"Thanks for the chocolate bars." Juan held one up and

examined it. He smiled. "Actually, I bought them for their medicinal properties," he said jokingly.

"They're free trade," Ben said. "The Scouts support people in third world countries and this time we are supporting a village in South America. That way they can make money and hopefully not chop down the rainforest."

Juan nodded. "Well, I've never had South American chocolate. I can't wait to try it."

Linda and Ben were heading out the front door when Linda reached into her purse and handed Juan her business card. "Why don't you stop by the nursing home? I manage the place. I'm looking for someone to help with basic chores. It's not very glamorous, and the pay isn't all that great, but if you think you might be interested while you figure out what you're going to do, this might be an option. I think having someone running around in a rabbit costume might be good for our residents."

Juan took the card and looked at it in disbelief. "Really?"

"Yes, we are shorthanded, and we were going to put an ad in the paper for an orderly."

"Thanks. When should I come by?"

"Come by tomorrow morning at 10:30. I'll have some time then. If it suits you, we can get you started right away."

Juan could not keep from smiling. He never thought he would be happy at someone offering him such a job. "You are very kind, Thank you. I'll see you in the morning."

21

Rabbit's Gotta Work

Juan arrived at the nursing home a little before 10:30 am. Unlike folks who might be content doing nothing, Juan couldn't stand being idle. He was eager to be productive. After his poor luck finding a job, he looked forward to doing whatever was needed at the nursing home, even though the pay was lousy.

Linda greeted him as he entered the lobby. "Well, hello, Juan. I see you made it."

"Are you kidding? I wouldn't miss it." He followed her to her office, and he saw some of the nursing home guests and the attendants moving about. He received a few smiles.

Linda showed Juan to her office and closed the door. "All right then, have a seat. As you might have guessed as we walked to my office, this is a constant care facility. Our guests are folks that cannot take care of themselves. Our staff helps our residents take care of everything from eating to going to the bathroom. All guests require constant supervision, and we do everything we can so they can live out the remaining part of their lives comfortably, with dignity and respect."

"What I need right now is an orderly to provide some basic care giving support to a few of our guests. Our attendants work in shifts, and all are trained. I realize that you are not, so you would be assigned to a supporting role, not a caregiver role. If you want to move up to become a caregiver you would need to be trained, but let's not get ahead of ourselves. This work is not for everybody. I thought you might be able to help me while you figure out what you are going to do, given your current situation. To be perfectly honest, I thought that someone running around in a rabbit costume might bring cheer to some of our guests. Many have reverted to a state that can best be described as childlike."

"I understand." He looked around her office and noticed the picture on her desk. "Is that Ben's father in that photo?"

She glanced at the photo, "Yes, that's Robert. He passed away two years ago."

"I'm really sorry. That Iraq war has been hard on a lot of families. It was his second tour of duty, wasn't it?"

She was surprised by his comment. "Yes, but how do you know that he was in the Iraq war and on his second tour? Did Ben mention something to you?"

Juan suddenly realized that he should not know all of that personal information. "I must apologize, Linda. Since my accident, physical contact with another person, like shaking hands, leaves me knowing much more about them than I can explain. It's as though I can see inside them. It just happens. When I shook your hand in the hospital, that's when I think I knew. It's usually followed by a short spell of dizziness. I'm sorry, Linda. I didn't mean to pry. I know that you loved him very much, and Ben also misses his dad a great deal."

Linda wiped her eyes. "We've been on our own for two years now. Yes, Ben misses his dad."

"He's a good kid, a natural born salesman." Juan pulled out one of the chocolate bars. "I had one of these, last night. They are really good."

Linda looked at the man in the rabbit costume holding up the chocolate bar and couldn't help but smile. She wiped her eyes again. "OK, funny man, let me show you what you'll be doing." She ran through the items he would do in his job. "Do you have any questions, Juan? Is this something that you think you might want to do?"

Juan nodded. "Yes, I'm sure. When can I start?"

She smiled. "Well, if you are ready, I can have you shadow Jackie today. She'll let you meet the guests whom you will be helping and show you around the place."

"I'm ready, Linda."

She paged Jackie and a few moments later, a short black woman in her mid-forties came in. "Jackie, I want you to meet Juan."

Jackie smiled and shook Juan's hand. He felt a little dizzy and instantly knew more about Jackie than he wanted to. Especially the part about how she was almost beaten to death by an abusive husband. She finally got the courage to walk out on the bum, and she took her daughter with her. She worked hard to send her daughter to a good private school and was currently working two jobs.

Jackie looked him up and down. "Good to meet ya. The folks here are just gonna luv you."

Juan spent the rest of the day with Jackie as she showed him what he was supposed to do. He could not help but feel better about himself after seeing how some of these folks were incapable of doing even the most basic things.

At lunch time, he went into the cafeteria with her and saw how the attendants helped the guests eat. Some were spoon-feeding their guests, just like you would feed a young child. Others were simply wiping their faces and standing by, assisting whenever they were needed. A few of the guests were talking. Most were quiet, and many had blank stares on their faces, as though they were lost and didn't know where they were. Juan could not help it. He got choked up seeing this and wiped away a tear from his eye.

Jackie noticed. "It still gets to me, too. Don't you worry none about that, you gotta good heart."

"We need to get lunch for Mr. Walters. He can't leave his room cause he's got to stay in bed for another day. He tumbled out of bed and bumped his head a couple of nights ago, and we are just being extra careful with him. Get yourself a tray, you can eat whiles I feed Mr. Walters. The food ain't bad, and you might as well get a bite since you gonna be busy the rest of the day. I usually eat whiles I help a guest. You get used to it."

Juan followed Jackie around the rest of the afternoon.

Linda caught up with them at one point to see how things were going. "Hi, Jackie, how's Juan doing?"

Jackie looked over at Juan. "Well, he ain't taken off yet, that's a good sign, and he's got a good feeling about him."

Juan looked at Linda. "Jackie's a pretty amazing lady. I'm

learning a lot from her today."

Linda smiled. "Yeah, she is pretty amazing. Before you leave, stop and see me on your way out." With that, Linda left them to continue his orientation.

Juan met the second of three guests that he would be assisting, and he watched as Jackie treated and tended to them as though they were her very own family. On their way to the last guest for the day, Juan asked, "So, how is your daughter doing at school?"

Jackie turned. "How do you know about my daughter?"

Juan then realized that he did it again. He was not supposed to know anything about her. "I think Linda may have mentioned something before you came to her office."

She still looked a little confused. "Oh, she's doing fine. She'll be graduating next year and wants to go to medical school. Child has big dreams. I pray to God every day that they'll all come true." She paused. "I didn't think Ms. Linda knew about my daughter. Oh well, Ms. Linda is a good lady. She really cares about the residents here."

Juan was relieved that he was able to get out of that without having to explain his rabbit touch.

They made their way to the last guest. "OK, this is Mr. Blake. He was just admitted yesterday. Poor man can't speak. He can barely move."

Juan headed to Linda's office after Jackie was through helping the new resident.

"So, Juan, how did you like your first day here?"

"This is a new world to me, Linda. Quite frankly, it will take me time to get used to it, but I am excited to be here. Under normal circumstances, I'm not sure I would have ever set foot into a place like this, but my circumstances are far from normal and I'm grateful to you for giving me a chance."

Linda was glad to hear it. "Well, you can officially start tomorrow, and you will be paid for today as well, but I would need you to work a Thursday through Monday schedule. You would be off Tuesday and Wednesday. Can you do that?

"That won't be a problem for me, Linda." Juan prepared to leave. "I'll see you in the morning."

22

The Emperor's New Clothes

Now that Monty was CEO, he felt that it was time for a wardrobe upgrade and a revamping of the CEO's office suite. After his morning workout with his personal trainer, Hernando, he decided to call Peggy and tell her he had important business out of the office.

He had to be the most eligible and attractive bachelor in the country. He was so pleased with his newfound power and status that he decided to visit McLamb's, the most exclusive tailor in the Southeast. There, he would pick out clothing that was worthy of his status and exquisite good looks. Besides, there were some board meetings coming up which required that he look the part and show the rest of those clowns that he meant business. Any talk or questioning his ability to run McPride Industries would be dealt with harshly.

Monty was glad to have John Delmont out of the way. He knew that John would be his most severe critic, so he had planned his opponent's early demise. John suspected nothing of what was coming. *"How could he?"* Monty thought, *"My brilliance is unparalleled. It's a gift, and why would I have such tremendous good looks, it if were not to use for my self-gratification?"*

A few days earlier, Monty visited Vanderbilt Village. He pretended to be a potential buyer and got a tour of unit 2A, located just below John Delmont's unit 3A. It was a newly constructed, three-story building that was part of an existing luxury living development. John was the first to occupy a unit in the new building.

After the tour, Monty asked the agent if he could look around a little more on his own and take pictures for his wife to see. The agent was more than happy to comply. She asked Monty to stop by the sales office on his way out.

Once he was alone, he looked around some more. He locked the unit door and pulled out a small high powered portable drill from his briefcase. He attached the high-strength bit along with the dust catcher, which attached to the front of the drill. The dust catcher looked like a small upside down umbrella.

He drilled two quarter-inch holes through the ceiling, one in the kitchen and one in the bedroom closet. He used a twelve inch bit to make sure that the holes went all the way through. Then, he wiped the areas clean of small amounts of stray debris and put the dirty paper towels into a small plastic bag. He then removed two small cylinders from his briefcase. He placed one of the compressed gas cylinders in the top kitchen cabinet and the other in the top shelf of the bedroom closet. He placed a small ignition device on the shelf in the kitchen cabinet which he would trigger by calling it with his cell phone.

Monty was particularly fond of gas explosions. They were so dramatic and colorful. He loved drama. In fact, after McPride Industries was running to his liking, he would take a trip to Hollywood. He was sure that he'd make a great actor. His apartment was decorated with framed posters of dramatic classics like Casablanca, Gone with the Wind, A Streetcar Named Desire, and others. He also loved theater and was a big fan of Andrew Lloyd Webber. He was particularly fond of the play Cats. He would enjoy performing in it, dressing up like a cat and dancing on stage. How liberating, he thought. If he had his pick, he would play Mr. Mistoffelees, the magical cat, and would probably receive standing ovations for it. For now, he would simply have to use his creative genius to help things go their proper way in the mundane world of McPride Industries.

Monty set the timer to 3:00 am. He was sure John Delmont would be asleep by then. The gas would slowly leak out of the canisters, and drift up through the small holes in the closet and kitchen cabinets. By 3:00 am the canisters would be empty. All the windows in unit 2A were sealed. The gas would be ignited easily.

He set his alarm to wake him up at 3:00 am.

Monty left the unit and stopped by the sales office. He thanked the sales lady and told her that he would look at a few more properties and let her know. He gave her a fake name and fake contact information.

Later that night, Monty's cell phone alarm went off. He rubbed his eyes, picked up the phone and dialed the series of numbers to ignite the gas. After doing so, he went back to sleep. John Delmont had no clue that his apartment would be blown up that night.

A couple of hours later, Monty got up, stretched, and had coffee before going to his morning workout with Hernando. He did not have to go far because Hernando occupied the guest bedroom of Monty's apartment.

Hernando came out of the bedroom and saw Monty sitting, having his coffee. They exchanged glances. Then Hernando turned on Monty's favorite song of all time, "YMCA." He clapped his hands and said in a heavy Spanish accent, "OK, Papi, cam' an let's go. Ju hav to staar moovings yu body."

Monty got up and joined Hernando in their morning workout. He was in a great mood. John Delmont was out of the picture. YMCA was playing. He looked good. He felt good. Life was great.

Today, Monty was eager to pick out some Italian fabrics for his new suit collection. He was measured and catered to by the McLamb staff. He pranced around trying on different styles of suits that would be used as patterns for his new collection. He loved looking at himself in the mirror as the tailors measured and pampered him. He thought he might try a different haircut, something a little more Leonardo DiCaprio.

After Monty's trip to McLamb's, he had his hair styled. Then he got a manicure, pedicure and facial. All in all, it was a productive day. His new wardrobe was picked out, one suit for each day of the week, for two weeks. At a cost just under $120,000, he figured that he was worth every penny.

Monty had dinner with Hernando. They went to the Cajun House and had some spicy, Louisiana style cooking to celebrate Monty's new wardrobe. Hernando approved of Monty's new haircut. At dinner, he complemented him. "Wow, papi, ju luk lika mubee estar." Then he blew a kiss. Monty blushed and told Hernando about his trip to McLamb's.

Monty described a couple of the fabrics that he picked out.

Hernando waved his hand. "No me diga, ju cracee gringo," and smiled.

Monty continued describing the rest of what he had selected.

Hernando sat there dreamy-eyed. At one point, he fanned himself with the menu, breathed a deep sigh. "No wey, aihh ayayay, I lov eet. I bet ju luk lik one big macho man."

Monty felt giddy, everything was going his way. He figured the world was full of stupid people. Since he was smarter than most, it was his responsibility to get what he wanted. He absolutely hated the weak and the poor. Most of them were just too stupid and lazy to think creatively like him.

Since he was a child, Monty had blown up quite a few things just for the fun of it. He bought a gun with a silencer at one point but felt his creativity lent itself better to blowing things up and torturing small, helpless animals, but what he enjoyed most was making people suffer. The weaker or needier they seemed to be, the more of a thrill it was to make their lives miserable. He particularly enjoyed his sneaky little spitting episodes. In a way, he felt that he was doing them a favor. He was much more than they could ever be. It was his little gift to them. Maybe some of his genius would rub off on them. They should be so lucky.

After a day of self-indulgence and partying with Hernando, Monty went to work the following morning. He liked his new role as CEO of McPride Industries. On his way into his office, Peggy greeted him, and announced that Edward Diaz, director of distribution, Milton Jacobs, director of pharma products, and Harold Ramirez, the chief financial officer, were waiting for him in his office.

Monty looked at her but maintained his composure. He raised an eyebrow. "Oh, I see. Well, I'd better see what the boys want." He entered his office and greeted them. "Gentleman, what can I do for you?" He took his seat behind the desk.

Harold Ramirez was the first to speak. "Monty, we wanted to talk to you about…"

Monty held up his hand in a stop gesture. "You will address me as Mr. McPride. Whatever your fears and insecurities may be, I will listen to them, but you will address me as Mr. McPride. Is that clear, gentlemen?" He looked around at each of them.

They each looked at one another. Ramirez paused for a moment then continued. "Very well, I will get straight to the point. As CFO, I have been asked to speak on behalf of the advisory board. We feel that you are not qualified to run this company and before our next meeting we wanted to give you the opportunity to step down on your own. The board has the highest respect and regard for your father, but we cannot accept this assignment of an unqualified person in a leadership position."

Monty sat silent for a moment. "I see." He looked at Harold. "So, the ungrateful advisory board would like to undo my father's last wish, based on a wild assumption that I am not qualified. I'm afraid that YOU, gentlemen, are mistaken. I am quite capable of running this company, but let's not argue the point. If this is the advice that I'm getting from my own advisory board, it is truly bad advice. You do realize that the advisory board is a non-voting entity that serves the CEO in his strategic planning for the future of this enterprise?"

"We realize that there is a great deal of risk to our personal careers in coming to you this way, but we decided it to be in the best interest of the company."

Monty looked at each of them, "Well, gentleman, I do respect your courage for coming to me in this way and would like to thank you. I would like to prove myself worthy of this position to each of you. Thank goodness, I don't have to. You're all fired!" He leaned forward in his chair. "Good day, gentlemen."

Ramirez protested, "You can't fire us. You're out of your mind. Do you realize the impact that this will have on the company?"

Jacobs rose from his chair. His cheeks were flushed. "This just proves our point! You are incapable of running this business. You're acting like a spoiled child. I suggest you reconsider your decision, Monty."

Monty gritted his teeth. "I asked you to call me Mr. McPride."

Edward Diaz, who had not spoken yet, stood up and shook

his finger at Monty. "Well, then, you should act like Mr. McPride. We've all given our best to this company and respect your father a great deal."

Monty was tired of this little revolt. "Don't you shake your finger at me. I'm not a schoolboy. Now, get out!" Then leaned over and buzzed Peggy. "Peggy, please see to it that Mr. Diaz, Jacobs, and the other one are escorted off the premises. They have been terminated, effective immediately. Have someone in HR make the appropriate arrangements to have them replaced."

"You're nothing but a fool." Ramirez had to control his impulse to ring Monty's neck. "You can never fill your father's shoes. You don't like what you hear, so you fire us? For crying out loud, man, you don't even know what each of us does. Keep making decisions like this one and your competition will be thanking you, and guess what? We'll be working for them."

"Good day, gentlemen." Monty went to the door and opened it, signaling that this meeting was over. The three men left Monty's office. He closed the door behind them, returned to his CEO chair and put his legs up on the desk. He took out a cigar and calmly smoked it. Monty felt better than giddy. He felt godlike.

After basking in his godlikeness for a while, Monty called McLamb's and told them that he needed at least one suit ready by the end of the day on Sunday, so he could wear it to work on Monday. The McLamb's tailor said it would be no problem and a small surcharge of $2,500 would be charged to his account.

Rush charges didn't concern him. This was a necessity. He needed to look his best to lead this simpleton staff that his father had organized to run the company. On Monday, he would start leading his flock. They would surely come to admire him over time and possibly even worship him, and with the three musketeers he fired now gone, there would be less chance for dissent among the troops.

After his phone call to McLamb's, he called Vivian's, a high end spa and hair salon located down the street. Since he was a frequent customer, he could get an appointment just about any time. He reached in his drawer for his copy of Cosmo and spoke to the customer service rep.

"Hello, this is Monty McPride. Do you have a copy of this month's Cosmo?"

"Why yes," replied the woman.

"OK, great, look at the featured model on the cover. Do you see her eyes?" Monty ran his finger over the picture.

"Yes, she is wearing a Ralph Lauren with the pearl necklace, absolutely gorgeous."

"Great, I need to come in for an eyelash extension. Can you do that?"

"Yes, absolutely, we have been doing quite a few recently. I see you have an appointment with us for Monday. Would you like to do it then?"

"No, no, no. I need to come in today. My Monday appointment is for my weekly massage."

"Yes, I see. Very well then, Sharon will see you this afternoon at 3:00 pm. Will that work?"

"Fantastic, see you then."

Monty decided to take the rest of the day off. He had done enough work for one day. Firing those idiots made his day. It was the best thing he could have done as the new CEO. No doubt the news would spread quickly among the staff, and no one else would bring up the subject. He wondered how he could be so unfairly gifted. Perhaps he really was a god.

23

Rabbits Welcome

Linda greeted Juan on his first official day working at the nursing home and they went over his duties. He would be assisting Jackie and another certified nursing assistant with various tasks. He wore plastic gloves to avoid prying into anybody's personal life in case he should touch them.

Early in the day, Juan helped change the beds of several guests. He helped Jackie clean up a urine spill in another room. He helped one of the guests comb his hair and helped a guest go to the bathroom. Jackie showed him how to clean a guest. Most of them were incapable of doing this for themselves.

At lunchtime, he was to take the newest resident, Blake McPride, to the cafeteria and feed him lunch. The old man had one of those lost gazes on his face. Although he could move, he had to be helped constantly with the most basic things. Feeding himself was something that he could not do. He was able to chew and swallow, but you had to feed him as you would feed a child.

The guests didn't even seem to notice that Juan was wearing a rabbit costume. That was comforting to him because, in a strange way, he was normal here. Juan sat patiently feeding Mr. Blake the carrots and peas. Then he would bring the cup of apple juice to the man's mouth and put the straw gently in Blake's mouth, at which time Blake would take small sips, almost as a reflex.

For dessert, he fed him applesauce. Juan nibbled on his

chocolate bar and put a couple of small pieces to the man's lips. *"Who doesn't like chocolate?"* he asked himself, feeling sorry for the man who couldn't have asked for it even if he wanted to.

Saturday was much the same, except for the fact that he gagged when he had to help one of the guests go to the bathroom. He tried holding his breath, but he ran out of time and almost fainted when he finally took a breath. Even with the smelliness of some of the things he had to do, Juan felt unusually at ease helping the guests. Maybe it was because he was really needed. Linda and Jackie appreciated what he did and he was not so busy thinking about his own plight. By now, he had started to get used to the fact that he was going to spend the rest of his life in the silly rabbit costume.

Juan had always been a practical person, just like his father had taught him to be. For most of his life, his jobs were inconsequential. His programming work, which he did very well, didn't really help anyone. It was something far removed from the kind of impact he felt he was now having on people. Some of them appeared to be lost inside themselves. In just two days, he had begun to gain a new appreciation for everything that he had. Apart from the rabbit issue, he was in relatively good health, had survived being electrocuted, was able to think and move about, and he was able to tend to his own personal hygiene without help from a stranger. He also possessed all of his limbs and senses, which seemed to be in good working order. He was thankful. He had never given those things much thought before. It was just the way things were.

Linda stopped by while he was making his rounds early on Saturday morning and asked him if he would like to join her and Ben for dinner that evening. He was so thrilled that he started to have conversations with the guests, though they were oblivious to him rambling on about things.

While he was feeding Mr. Blake, Juan rattled on, "Can you believe it, Blake? Linda invited me to dinner later tonight. She has a great kid for a son. Ben is a Boy Scout, a really great kid. He even saved my life a few days ago. How about that, Blake?" Then Juan pretended to have a conversation. "So, you don't like the soggy carrots? Well, I don't blame you. I know, I know. You wish you could have some pecan pie for dessert today, but all I see is not-so-happy jello. Oh wait, here's Mr. Chocolate bar to save the day. Good isn't it? Yeah, I know, what did I tell you. Ben sold me twelve of these. I'm down to my last five. Don't worry, good buddy. I will try to get more."

Later that evening, Juan enjoyed a meal of Chinese food at Linda's house. She asked him about his first day on the job and she let him know that if he needed to leave, for whatever reason, that would be OK, but that he was doing a great job with the guests, and she hoped that he would want to stay.

After dinner, Juan went home and found a large envelope on the kitchen table. He opened it and saw the divorce papers. On it was a note from Leigh.

Juan,

Please sign these and put them in the mail. Since we have separate bank accounts and there is nothing to argue over, I'm sure you won't have a problem with these papers. The lawyer said that an uncontested divorce could be expedited, and we should be legally divorced by next Friday.

And guess what? Great news! Bill and I are getting married! Thanks for being a good sport about all of this. I hope there are no hard feelings.

Leigh

Juan put down the papers and thought for a moment about how he was feeling. He would have expected himself to be angry and sad, but he felt neither. He sat there for a couple of minutes waiting for a delayed reaction of heartbroken disappointment, but none came. He then reached for a pen and signed the papers. He put them in the stamped, self-addressed envelope that was enclosed. He would put them in the mailbox first thing Monday.

As he sat at the kitchen table, more memories surfaced of the time he spent with Leigh. He remembered how sometimes she would speak louder than anybody he knew. She had a tendency to make a grand entrance whenever they attended a social function. She would enter the room talking at the top of her voice, almost yelling. It was as though she had a Leigh alarm that announced the arrival of the life of the party. She wanted everybody to know that she was on the premises, and the good times could begin. It had never really bothered him until now.

He also remembered how she would throw in a cliché or two whenever she was on a roll being the life of the party. Aside from how they met, at the wine tasting party, and their intense but brief physical attraction, he really had nothing in common with her. He thought that marriage was the right thing at the time, but now he wondered if this divorce could really be something he needed but had been too blind or numb to see.

The more he thought of it, the more he realized there were signals and occurrences that should have made him think, but he never paid much attention. He continued living his life, accepting the numbness as normal.

More revelations came to him, such as how intensely he disliked it when she spoke baby talk and acted all cutesy in public when they were together. He thought it amusing at first. Eventually, he didn't think much of it at all. Now he thought it was idiotic. She also had an irritating habit of buying things in bulk, even when they didn't have room for it. Paper towels were her favorite bulk purchase item.

Why was he thinking about all of this? *"Why did I not see this more clearly before now?"* He wondered. *"Was it possible that I thought so little of myself that I subjected myself to being married to the most self-centered woman in the world?"* Now that he thought of it, every conversation that was not about Leigh usually met a swift end or was masterfully turned to become about her. He had never really paid much attention to that until now.

Juan looked at himself in the mirror and thought, *"Could being sentenced to a life in a rabbit costume have liberated me in some weird way?"*

He sat back down. *"This is the first time in a long time that I feel a sense of purpose and actually feel happy. How can that be? Could I really feel happy after all that has happened? What if Ben hadn't come to the door when he did?"*

All of a sudden the phone rang and Juan saw that it was Angie calling. "Hi, Sis."

"Juan, I just want to see how you're doing and wanted to invite you to come to the 5:30 Mass tomorrow and dinner afterwards. It's been a while. Are you up to it?"

Juan glanced at the envelope containing the divorce papers. "I guess I am up to it. Are you and Ray still attending St. Paul's?"

"The same one. Why don't we meet you there at quarter past five? Are you sure you're up to it, Juan?"

"Yes, I'm sure. I'll see you there."

"OK, love you."

"Love you too, Sis."

Juan cleaned up his apartment. He even cleaned his closet and found the box containing his old photos and a wrinkled piece of paper that he had saved all these years. He read the letter he had written to National Geographic all those years ago when he thought anything was possible. Why did he allow life to rob him of his dreams? Why hadn't he pursued photography? How much time had he wasted, living as a drone in a meaningless existence?

He remembered how he loved to take pictures as a kid. It was like magic. What had happened to him all those years ago to convince him that the numbness in his heart was the way things were supposed to be? He came across his old film camera, picked it up and held it for a moment. He thought back to the joy he felt when the light was just right, and the shot was his and his alone. Then his eyes swelled up with tears, and they began to flow as he clung to his old camera.

That night, ten minutes before the store was scheduled to close, Juan walked into his local electronics store and purchased a high quality 35 mm digital camera. He received strange looks, and there was always somebody with a wise crack about how he was dressed, but it didn't seem to bother him. He wound up making friends with the people in line and when he stepped up to the cashier, it seemed to brighten her mood.

Maybe looking so wacky in a rabbit outfit was making people stop and look for a moment. Maybe it was forcing them to smile in spite of themselves.

After work the following day, Juan met Angie, Ray, and the two boys at church. David and Matthew enjoyed their crazy uncle in the rabbit costume. During Mass, it was hard to keep them from looking at Juan and smiling at one another. Other kids also seemed a bit distracted, wondering what the Easter Bunny was doing in the church today.

It had been awhile since Juan last attended Mass. He listened as Fr. Jerry gave the homily. He talked about "charisms" and how they are gifts from God to be used to build God's kingdom on earth, to help one another. He talked about how God doesn't always give us what we want, but always provides us with what we need.

He mentioned the man who was born blind until Jesus rubbed mud in his eyes and gave him back his sight. The thing that struck Juan about the homily was when Fr. Jerry told the congregation that after Jesus restored the man's sight, the local authorities became upset because he had performed a miracle on the Sabbath, which was supposed to be a day of rest. They were so hung up on maintaining the letter of the law that they lost sight of the larger picture.

"How crazy is that?" Juan thought. *"I've been maintaining my numb existence and missing the big picture, the fulfilling life that is mine to make."*

Then it hit Juan. *"I've been on my own this whole time. I've been lonely my entire life. Maybe that's why I was so eager to marry Leigh, to fill that hole. Maybe that's why I longed to go to church when I was a child even though my father was a devout atheist. Perhaps I have always known that there was something more to life but never quite connected the dots. It never occurred to me to ask God for guidance. I've built my own little numb life, with my limited expectation of what was possible. Maybe this ridiculous rabbit costume is the mud that Jesus has put in my eyes."* Juan thought about this as he stood with Angie, Ray, David and Matthew, holding hands and saying the Lord's Prayer. After they had finished praying, Juan muttered to himself, *"Thank you, Jesus. Now that I've found you, I'm not letting go."*

After Mass, some of the parishioners came up to Juan and asked him why he was dressed that way. He explained in as few words as possible the fact that it was related to a medical condition. Some folks thought it amusing. Others didn't know how to respond. A few told him that he shouldn't come to church dressed that way. Others only smiled and called their children. Juan was attracting a bigger crowd than the priest.

Ray looked at his watch. "I think it's time we head home."

Angie had prepared a pot of stew in the slow cooker. The

smell filled the house. When they entered, everyone took a deep breath. There were multiple "mmmm's" as each experienced the wonderful, mouthwatering aroma.

The kids both asked, "When do we eat?" It was a simultaneous chorus which they would repeat several times before dinner.

They spent time playing with their uncle Juan and each had plenty of questions for him about what it was like to look funny all the time. They also wanted to know if it hurt when he had his accident and what would happen if he took the costume off.

During dinner, Juan told Ray and Angie all about his new job and the woman who recommended he try it until he figured out what he wanted to do. He described his work, excluding details of bathroom duty. Then Juan asked Ray how his job was going.

Ray looked up. "Not too good, I'm afraid. The new guy in charge is a jerk, and I'm convinced that he had something to do with sending his father to the hospital. Now he wants the formula which we have been developing, which is legally his, but I just have a feeling that he is up to no good. He's arrogant and does the grossest things, which I won't bother sharing since we are eating. I think the guy is a mental case. He's a spoiled brat, and he's a creep."

Juan smiled. "Sounds like a classmate I had when I was a kid in school. He was a rich kid and nasty as could be."

Ray continued, "Anyway, he's threatened to fire our firm from the account unless we give him the completed formula. It's completed, but I've been holding out, hoping that I could turn up some evidence to prove my suspicion."

"Have you found anything?"

"No," admitted a disappointed Ray. "I guess tomorrow I will just hand the formula over to this maniac and hope we are allowed to stay on the account."

Angie paused and looked at her husband. "Why don't you go to the police and tell them what you suspect?"

"That wouldn't do any good. There was nothing suspicious about it, so no one had bothered to investigate. Besides, even if the police did get involved, I'm sure that any incriminating evidence is long gone by now. This guy is a slick operator."

Juan had a flashback to his childhood years. "Yeah, so was

my schoolmate from hell."

Ray didn't want to talk about work. He changed the subject. "So, you like the Scout's mom, Juan?"

"Yeah, she's a very caring person."

"That's not what I mean, Juan. Do you like the Scout's mom?"

This time Juan blushed a bit and looked over at Angie. "I've just met her, and it was kind of by accident, but she is very attractive, I must admit."

Angie was surprised that Juan could even think of anybody besides Leigh, especially after the way he reacted to her note. "What about Leigh?"

Juan told her about the divorce papers that Leigh left for him along with the note, which included a marriage announcement.

"So, you're not upset as you were the other night when you wound up in the hospital?"

Juan could hear the concern in her voice. She was afraid that he might resort to taking his suit off again. "No, I'm not upset. I think this is for the best. I wish her well. This dumb rabbit costume has saved me from being married to someone whom I do not love. I wasn't sure of that until yesterday. I should have listened to you, Angie. You've had a relationship with Jesus for a while now. Both you and Ray have allowed him into your life. I was a fool. It's taken this crazy accident to show me that I am not alone, and it's not all about me. I am certain that I'll be fine. In fact, I bought a camera yesterday. I haven't felt this good in a long time."

Angie was relieved to hear it. She had been worried that he would fall into a state of depression over all of this and spend the rest of his life as a bitter, frustrated and lonely man.

"Ray, the children, and I have been praying for you, Juan. We've been really praying that God would show you the way. I can't tell you how happy I am to hear that you are doing all right in spite of everything that has happened to you. It would be easy to fall into depression and get stuck there." She smiled and came over and gave him a kiss on the cheek. "Perhaps at some point, we can meet Linda. She sounds like a terrific lady. I mean if anything develops, that is."

Juan smiled. "You will be the first to know, little sister."

24

Manic Monday

Ray received a call from Peggy first thing in the morning to inform him that Mr. McPride would meet with him at 4:00 pm instead of 9:00 am. Ray was a little relieved, but nothing was apt to change between now and then. He still had nothing for the police.

Monty had more important things to do this morning. For one thing, his new suit needed adjusting. It was a little too loose on the back side, and he was sure that it made his behind look big. This was unacceptable. So he spent the morning at McLamb's, telling them exactly how he wanted the suit altered. He went shopping for a new briefcase. The one he had cried "boring."

By the time he got back to McLamb's at around noon, everything was altered to his specifications. He put on his new suit and headed to the office. He would take care of whatever nonsense needed his attention or required the CEO's signature. Then he would be off to Vivian's for his weekly massage. Ray Cromwell would have to adjust his schedule and accommodate the CEO's more pressing itinerary.

Juan arrived at work and got right into his routine, which was slightly different every day. That was one of the things he enjoyed. He didn't know exactly what to expect. His help was needed in different situations. His only regular predictable duty was lunch time with Blake, which he also enjoyed. There was something therapeutic about talking to someone who could not talk back. It was the complete opposite of having a conversation with

Leigh, which always resulted in some self-glorifying story.

Today, lunch featured the usual carrots, peas, and some turkey and gravy. For dessert, there were peeled pears. Juan talked to Blake as he had now gotten used to doing. "Well, the turkey and gravy aren't bad. I don't know about you, but I don't much care for pears."

He fed a few spoons full of the soft pears to the old man and then whispered, "Not to worry, old buddy. I have Mr. Chocolate with us today. Sadly, tomorrow will be the last time I can bring him. I am down to two bars, but do not despair. I will go directly to the source and get us some more." He shared a piece of chocolate with Blake.

After lunch, he picked up the food tray and brought it over to the sink. He removed his gloves and washed his hands. As he was drying them, he glanced at Blake. The old man was keeling over to the side like a drunk falling off a stool after too much to drink. He was going to hit the floor.

Juan gasped and ran over to the chair and reached him just in time to prevent the leaning tower of Blake from crashing down. "That's all I need is for you to slide off your chair and break your neck. Thank God, I was able to catch you in time." Juan put him in his wheelchair. Then he started to head back to the sink for a new pair of plastic gloves, but he had to sit down. It was too late. He was hit with a wallop of a dizzy spell. "Crap! My gloves, I shouldn't have taken them off."

A few moments later, after the dizziness passed, Juan opened his eyes and looked at Blake McPride up close. "Man oh man, it's really you!"

Juan took Blake McPride back to his room and sat him in his recliner as usual. He didn't want the old man sliding off his chair, especially since he had to find Linda right away. He tucked him into the chair and rushed down the hallway, crashing into Jackie on his way.

"I'm sorry, Jackie," he yelled as he got up and continued to run down the hall.

Jackie yelled back, "I thought you liked it here." Then she shook her head, "Oh well, he must have had to clean up after Mr. Hastings."

Juan wasn't looking where he was going and nearly ran

into an old woman in a wheelchair. As she flinched at the impending collision, Juan stopped short and did a flip over her chair as though he had been thrown over the handle bars of a bicycle. The old woman smiled as the crazy bunny did his flip and then she applauded.

Juan quickly got up. "Whoops, sorry about that, you all right?" He continued to run frantically. Finally, he reached Linda's office. She stood up as he ran in.

"Juan, what in the world's the matter? Are you all right?" She took him and helped him sit in one of the two guest chairs. She sat in the other one. "Juan, tell me what's happened."

Juan pointed to the door. "Mr. Blake."

"Oh my God, is he hurt?" She cried as she stood up, heading for the door.

Juan grabbed her arm while shaking his head. He swallowed. "No, Blake is all right, but I know who tried to kill him."

Linda was stricken with apparent shock. "What? What do you mean, tried to kill him? Who?"

"His son, Monty McPride tried to kill him. Blake was leaning to one side at lunch. I was at the sink and saw him beginning to topple, so I ran and caught him as he was about to fall out of his chair. I guess I must have touched him long enough to get flooded with what was in his mind. I got really dizzy and then it all hit me, just like when you and I shook hands in the hospital."

"Oh my goodness, Juan, what are we going to do?"

Juan looked anxiously at Linda. "I hope you know that I'm not crazy, but I have to warn my brother-in-law. He has a meeting with this lunatic today. For now, that's all I can think of doing."

Juan dialed Ray's cell phone. It seemed to take forever for Ray to pick up. "Ray, you're not going to believe this, but I know Monty McPride tried to murder Blake McPride."

Ray was quiet for a moment. *"Juan, how do you know this? I never mentioned my client's name to you."*

"It's a long story, Ray. I knew you would want to know. You said you had a meeting with him today. I thought I'd warn you. Did you meet with him yet?"

"No, he rescheduled our meeting for this afternoon at four. I'm coming to the nursing home. I know where it is, and I'm not

too far."

Juan and Linda went to check on Mr. Blake. He was still in his chair, just the way Juan had left him. Linda called Scott, another assistant, and asked that he tend to Blake McPride.

As they were returning to Linda's office, Ray entered the lobby.

Juan waved. "This way, Ray." The three of them sat in Linda's office.

Ray looked at his brother-in-law. "You haven't gone off the deep end, have you, Juan?"

"No, I haven't gone off the deep end, not quite yet. When I was helping Mr. Blake with his lunch, I touched him accidentally and was able to see what was in his mind. I saw what happened. Blake never suspected that his own son would try to kill him."

Ray looked at Juan, now convinced that he really was crazy.

"Juan, come on. Do you expect me to believe that you read the man's mind? I know you have been through a lot lately, but you seemed fine yesterday."

"I'm fine, Ray. It's been happening since the accident. When I have physical contact with someone, there is some kind of transfer that happens, and I know what they know and what they have experienced. It's like a Vulcan mind meld on *Star Trek*."

Ray could not help but laugh. "You're nuts. This whole accident has been a lot harder on you mentally than I thought. Juan, just think about this logically. You were at my house yesterday, and we shook hands. You didn't have any close encounter of the Ray kind."

"I have not had physical contact with you ever since the accident. I didn't shake your hand yesterday. I gave you a hug and patted you on the back. There was no skin to skin contact. At church, I held David and Matthew's hand. I did get a dose of what's in their heads, but it was innocent enough. I did not want to hold hands with any adult at church. I didn't shake anyone's hand, and here I have been wearing plastic gloves since I started working to make sure I didn't accidentally pry into someone's mind."

Ray squinted his eyes, not sure what to think. He looked at Linda. She nodded.

Juan continued, "I shook Linda's hand at the hospital and

connected with her that way. I've apologized to her for doing so. It was quite by accident. It was how I discovered that Leigh had an affair." Juan sat down.

Ray was silent for a moment as he thought of how Angie would feel to know that her brother was mentally ill. "I'm sorry, Juan. I don't mean to doubt you, but it's just that this sounds too weird. It's…"

Juan got up from his chair. "I'm not crazy, Ray. Here, give me your hand." Ray looked at Juan, wondering if he should do so or not. *"Could Juan become violent?"*

"C'mon, Ray. If I'm a nut case, you'll know it in five minutes. Then you can get me psychological help." Juan looked at Linda and gave her a wink. She looked as though she wasn't too sure herself. Ray reluctantly extended his hand. Juan stepped back toward the chair.

"I'm going to sit down first because I usually get dizzy afterwards. OK, give me your hand."

"All right, but I want you to know that you are freaking me out."

Juan took Ray's hand. After ten-seconds, he let go and closed his eyes. Ray and Linda looked at each other, hoping that Juan was not crazy.

Juan opened his eyes. He stared at the floor for a few seconds. Then he got up from his chair and looked at Ray. "You had a big, greasy cheeseburger for lunch on Friday, and you feel guilty for lying to Angie about going off your diet, especially after the doctor told you that you that your cholesterol was high. The username to KC's handheld device is Superfly. The password is 4MoeLarry&Curly, and you recently rented the movie, 'Shaft.'"

Ray's jaw became unhinged. "How do you know that?"

"I don't know how I know, Ray. It's some bizarre side effect from the accident. That's one of the reasons Leigh left. The rabbit costume was bad enough. Then she told me I had turned into a mind reading freak."

Ray was still processing all the he had just heard. "Well, you've got to admit, that is rather freaky."

"Yeah well, when I touched Mr. McPride to keep him from falling out of his chair, I got a rush of his recent memories. Monty most definitely tried to kill him. That's how he wound up in the condition he's in. Monty wanted to run the company. He came into his office and forced him to sign some paperwork making Monty the successor. He tried to blackmail the old man by withholding his medicine. Then he stuffed a rag in Blake's mouth and waited for his heart to give out, but Peggy, the secretary, walked in and found Monty leaning over the old man's body. Lucky thing she did and called 911."

Ray nodded as he paced a few steps. "Up to now, everyone thinks that Blake McPride had some kind of stroke as a result of not taking his medicine, but it was attempted murder by his own son? You know, Juan, I suspected something. I just knew that lunatic had something to do with it."

Linda put one hand up to her mouth. "Oh my goodness, what a horrible man! How could he do such a thing?"

Ray thought of his encounters with McPride, Jr. "Monty is an evil man. I saw him do some gross things while on my way out of the McPride offices, and he treats people with disdain. He believes himself to be a superior being."

"Ray, do you remember me mentioning a classmate from hell last night during dinner? Well, Monty's the guy. I can't believe he's back in my life again. He scared the crap out of me when I was a kid. At one point, he left a dead squirrel in our mailbox and he threatened to hurt Angie if I didn't let him use my photo for a contest in school, which he won. I know firsthand that he is a lunatic. He's always been a bully, and I'm afraid he might get away with this if we don't do something."

Linda had an idea: "Why don't we call the police and you can tell them what you've told us? Between what you and Ray know, they would have to do something."

Juan put a finger to his chin. "Let's see, the police are going to take the word of a grown man dressed up like a rabbit who claims he can read people's minds accusing the new CEO of McPride Industries of attempted murder?" Juan paused. "Linda, I just don't think that's going to work. You can see how my own brother-in-law thought I was nuts. Can you imagine what the police will think?" He thought for a moment of what he saw in Blake's mind. Then he came up with an option. "There is something we might be able to do to get the police to listen."

"Yeah? What?" Ray was eager to hear it, whatever it was.

Juan recounted more of what he learned when he touched Blake. "The old man had a hidden recording device in his office. If we can get hold of it, we can turn the evidence over to the police. I don't think anybody else knew about it."

"Are you sure?" Ray hoped it was really true.

"Yeah, I'm sure. I saw it. It's concealed in his desk lamp. He's had it there for a while. It's voice activated when you say the words, 'call security.'"

Linda looked at Juan. "You can't get into Monty's office!"

Ray agreed. "No, but maybe I can. I am scheduled to meet with him regarding the BD109 bonding agent. I would have to get there early, and have enough time to look around. I'm sure Peggy, his secretary, would let me in."

"When is your meeting?" Juan asked.

"At four this afternoon; it's almost noon. I'll send Peggy a text. Hopefully, she can respond shortly."

He typed a brief note and sent it asking her to call him ASAP. She would call him when it was safe to talk. A few minutes later, Ray's phone buzzed.

"Hi, Peggy, are you able to talk freely?"

"*Yes,*" she replied. "*I'm running a couple of errands before getting some lunch. What's up, Ray?*"

"Do you know if Monty plans on being in his office before my meeting with him this afternoon?"

"*He has a three o'clock appointment at Vivian's. He goes there every week for a back massage and spa treatment. He will come back to the office at four to meet with you. Ray, I still haven't been able to find anything about what happened to Blake.*"

"Don't worry about that, Peggy. I have reason to believe that Blake McPride had some kind of recording device in his office. I would ask you to look for it, but I don't want you to risk getting caught. I suspect Monty has his own surveillance system deployed throughout the building. Since my meeting is at four, I thought I could wait for him in his office pretending to be getting paperwork ready for him. I could look around and not stir up any suspicion. Do you think we can swing that?"

"*I think so. I know that he is eager to meet with you.*"

"Thanks Peggy. See you at three."

"*OK. Bye.*"

Ray turned to Juan and Linda. "Well, at least now we have a plan. If the recorder is there, we'll get it this afternoon. Monty will be at Vivian's getting a spa treatment and I will snoop around his office before my meeting with him. Juan, I need you to go to Vivian's and keep an eye on him and call me when he leaves. It is just a short walk from the office, so I want to be ready just in case I'm busy looking for it, or just in case I'm in the middle of removing it."

Juan nodded. He thought that was a good plan. Linda told Juan to be extra careful so he wouldn't be spotted by Monty on his way back. He promised Linda that he would be very careful.

"OK, Juan, I'm going to head back to my office to prepare some papers for my meeting. You should be in position near Vivian's by three so that you can confirm when he has entered and warn me when he leaves. It would be safer to text me updates. Only call me if it's an emergency."

Ray headed to his office to get the necessary documents. Juan headed back to check on Blake. He had a while before he needed to get into position near Vivian's.

Juan pulled up a chair and sat down in front of Blake. "I know what happened to you. Ray, my brother-in-law, and I are going to try to get the evidence. When I was a kid, you came to my house. You had just moved into our neighborhood. The mailman delivered my first copy of National Geographic to your house by mistake. I was so excited to get my first issue. I've got to be honest, though. I was relieved when I found out that you had moved into your new house, and Monty would not be coming back to our school. He wasn't nice to anybody, especially to me and my sister. I can't imagine what you must be feeling, if you can feel anything at all, but we're going to try to get the evidence that will reveal the truth of what happened."

Juan got up to leave the room.

Linda was standing in the doorway. "That poor man, it must be awful to think that his son tried to kill him. Be careful, Juan. Call me when you find something." They left the room, but neither of them saw the tear running down the left side of Blake McPride's face.

25

The New Improved Monty

Monty was a block from the office. He walked like a peacock with full swagger. He couldn't help looking at himself in the glass of the various businesses as he approached McPride headquarters. He grinned to himself because he was a much better dressed and much better looking version of John Travolta during the opening sequence of *Saturday Night Fever*. He played the music in his head as he walked down the street.

He entered McPride Headquarters, took off his sunglasses and shook his hair, like a model walking down a runway. He noticed how people admired him. He walked up to the front counter receptionist just for fun and said, "How are you doing today?" He gave her a smile.

She cheerfully replied, "Fine, sir."

He winked at her and continued on his exhibition walk. He knew that she must want him. From the way she looked at his eyes, she must think he was a full-fledged dreamboat, which he was. In fact, Monty believed that he must be the most interesting man in the world.

As he entered the elevator, he noticed how everyone in the lobby watched the doors close. It was as if he had just come off stage at a big production and the audience was eagerly waiting for his return, for his next big scene. He was happy to bring joy to these ordinary and dull people. He stepped off the elevator and approached Peggy's desk.

He greeted her with a grin. "Good afternoon, Peggy."

Peggy looked up. "Good afternoon, Mr. McPride."

He leaned over close to her and whispered, "Do you like what you see, Peggy?" Then he backed away from the desk and twirled like a model doing a photo shoot. She looked and gave the nut a smile. "Yes, Mr. McPride. You look quite handsome."

He came a little closer. "Do you see anything different?"

She looked him over. "Well, I see that you are wearing a beautiful new suit, and your hair is different. You look good."

He put his face within a few inches of her face. "Come on. Don't you see anything else different about me?" Then he smiled.

"Well, let's see." She leaned back to put a little distance between their faces as she tried to figure out what he was getting at. "Oh, I see. Are you wearing some mascara?"

Monty put his hand on his hips. "No, you silly goose, I got my eyelashes extended." Then he got close to her again. "See?" She backed up as he stuck his face close to hers again, not wanting to be obvious about it. He took a deep breath. "Who needs me today, Peggy?"

She looked at her notes. "HR needs to talk to you about replacements for Ramirez, Jacobs, and Diaz. Mr. Pomeroy, our head of marketing, would like to meet with you about campaigns that will be running for several of our higher-end surgical items. We received a call from Finance, and they want to meet with you about many issues that are pending now that we have no CFO. Distribution would also like to know how to proceed. They are receiving calls and complaints since no order acknowledgments have gone out since yesterday, and the board of directors has called for an emergency meeting tomorrow morning. They would like you to attend since you were not at this morning's meeting."

Monty rolled his eyes. "What are these people, incompetent? I fire three people in a business that employs hundreds, and nobody can function? It's a wonder my old man didn't die of a heart attack earlier."

"Oh yes, and your father was moved to the new total care nursing facility. There was nothing more the hospital could do, so they moved him there. You'll have to sign some papers."

All of a sudden Monty looked a little worried. "Has there been any change in his condition?"

"No, sir."

Monty sighed. "Good! ... I mean it's good that they moved him to the new facility. I'll have to pay him a visit soon. He probably won't live very long, I'm afraid."

Peggy did not respond.

After a momentary pause in the conversation, Monty smiled. "Very well, I'll deal with my little flock after I get back from my massage appointment this afternoon and my meeting with that annoying Mr. Cromwell. He seems to have quite a paranoid imagination, you know. He rambles on about some kind of coffee conspiracy. Has he mentioned anything to you about it, by any chance?"

She looked up at him. "No, he hasn't mentioned anything about a coffee conspiracy to me."

"Well, that's good. I don't think Mr. Cromwell will be with us much longer, and it's probably for the best." He went into his office and closed the door. A few minutes later Fred Wilkins arrived at Monty's office and gave a polite knock.

"Come in. Have a seat," Monty instructed with a friendly gesture. "Fred, you've been my little helper, and I mean to reward you for your clever and creative ways of manipulating information, embezzling funds and other necessary duties to get the old geezer out of here, including disabling his little buzzer. Now, I have another important task for you."

Wilkins felt like the teacher's pet. He knew that he and Monty were a real team. Monty relied on him for quite a few things, and now he had another task to entrust to him.

"Anything, Monty," Fred responded, like an eager schoolboy.

Monty put up his hand. "Mr. McPride. You need to address me as Mr. McPride. I am, after all, the CEO of this company and we don't want to appear to be too chummy."

Fred looked like a hurt child. "Yes, of course, Mr. McPride."

Monty gave him a condescending smile. "I need you to devise a way to incriminate Hopkins as the one who falsified the company records. Just in case some eager beaver starts snooping around, I want a trail that leads to Hopkins."

In spite of being a sleazebag, Wilkins felt that Hopkins was not a good choice as the fall guy. "Hopkins is a hardworking family man. He has a wife and four kids. Can't we point the evidence to someone else? There would be prison time if anyone ever bothered to follow the evidence trail. His kids won't have a father anymore."

"Don't be ridiculous," Monty snapped. "That's perfect. Where's your sense of fun, Wilkins? Let me know when you've completed whatever it is that you have to do to point the finger at Hopkins. Then we will discuss your promotion."

"OK, Monty. I mean, Mr. McPride."

A few moments later, Wilkins exited Monty's office. Fifteen minutes later, Monty emerged.

"Peggy, I need you to compile a list of all the black employees who work at this office. You do not need to bother HR with it. I want you to compile it personally. Is that clear?"

She looked up at him somewhat concerned. "Why would you need a list like that?"

He smiled, then snapped his fingers and wiggled his neck from side to side. "I juz got some biznezz wit my homies. Next week, you can compile the list of all the Hispanics." With that, he gave her a wink, "Comprende?" He turned and did his best Saturday Night Fever walk to the elevator. "I'll be back in time to meet with Mr. Cromwell and he'd better have what I need."

After Monty had gotten in the elevator, Peggy went to the ladies room and texted Ray.

26

Mission Impossible

Ray was waiting in the lobby of the building across the street from McPride Industries. When he received Peggy's text message, he stood watch until he saw Monty's flamboyant emergence into the street. He looked as though he was participating in his own fantasy. His walking seemed contrived, and he kept raising his sunglasses and looking at his reflection in the glass as he walked toward Vivian's.

Ray called Juan and told him that Monty was on his way. Juan was waiting in the lobby of the building, which hosted some health and fitness stores. There was a drugstore and a nutrition store located directly across the lobby from Vivian's. There was a gym next door.

Juan was standing in the drugstore area. He wore a raincoat, an enormous black wig which covered all but the top third of his bunny ears. He wore a pair of large sunglasses and red lipstick. He looked like Hugh Hefner's worst nightmare, a fat middle-age playboy bunny with a beard shadow. Unlike the smiles he was accustomed to getting when dressed as a rabbit, people now seemed to avoid looking at him. Ironically, Juan was standing next to an eye drops display, pretending to be checking his email. He saw Monty enter the building and walk into Vivian's. Juan waited until he could see him go into the back. Then he called Ray and told him the coast was clear.

Ray arrived at Peggy's desk and they both play acted in

case they were being recorded.

"Good afternoon, Peggy."

"Good afternoon, Mr. Cromwell."

Ray smiled. "I'm here for my four o'clock meeting with Mr. McPride. I realize I'm a bit early. Is there a space I can use to organize my presentation for him? I know he is a busy man."

Peggy stood up, "Why of course, Mr. Cromwell. Just follow me. Why don't you prepare the papers in Mr. McPride's office? He is out at the moment." She was about to walk him to Monty's office when Fred Wilkins approached her.

"Excuse me, Peggy. Mr. McPride asked me to fix something in his office while he is out. It shouldn't take long." He then opened the office door and went in and shut it behind him.

Peggy and Ray looked at each other. Each thought the same thing *"Now what?"*

Ray took a seat in the waiting area, and Peggy returned to her desk. They each glanced at the clock and sat silently waiting for Fred Wilkins to finish whatever he was doing. Time ticked; Ray waited. Peggy and Ray occasionally glanced at one another. She shrugged her shoulders as if to say, "I don't know what he's doing in there so long."

Finally, the door to Monty's office opened, and Fred Wilkins emerged. "All done." He waved and left.

It was now a quarter to four and Ray noticed that he was sweating. Peggy stood up and pointed to the open office. "Mr. Cromwell, if you would like to prepare for your meeting, you can do so in Mr. McPride's office."

Ray stood up at once. "Thank you." He walked into Monty's office and shut the door. He knew that he was probably on surveillance, so he acted like he was really preparing for the meeting. He looked carefully at the surface of the desk and studied what was on it. There was nothing of consequence except for a copy of Cosmo.

Ray spread several papers out on the desk in an organized fashion and saw the small lamp on the desk. It was turned off. He looked around at the overhead lights as though he was thinking that he needed more. Then, he slowly reached for the small lamp, studying it closely as he reached for it. He pretended not to know where the on-off switch was located. This allowed him to study it more carefully. Then he turned it on. *"Nothing here."* He went to the window and opened the blinds some more. He studied everything in the office. He returned to the desk, leaned over the paperwork and pretended to be reading them. All the while, he was scoping the rest of the office. Then Ray sat in the guest chair and took out his phone. He covered the screen to hide his typing from any hidden cameras.

"Cant find it. wer shuld I lok"

A moment later, he received a reply text from Juan.

"Lamp on desk or wall has to b ther."

Ray looked around the room again. He retraced slowly and intensely looked at everything in the room. *"Nothing, but it has to be here. Maybe Juan just imagined the existence of the device. Perhaps he was a little crazy after all,"* Ray was sweating profusely.

Then Ray received another text from Juan.

"Almost dun here"

He replied.

"Need mor tim cant fnd it"

A moment later, Juan entered Vivian's. The woman at the counter looked like she had just come face to face with Godzilla. Juan smiled, lowered his sunglasses.

"Relax, I work with Monty and some of us are playing a practical joke on him. He is always joking with us. I'm supposed to surprise him. Is he still getting his back massaged?"

"Yes, he has three more minutes."

Juan smiled. "OK, hon, I'd better move quickly then. How do you like my outfit?" The women at the counter laughed and pointed at the third door down the hall. Juan entered the room and saw Monty lying on his stomach while one of the massage therapists worked on his back. Monty was groaning in delight as she worked his muscles. The therapist turned around and looked at Juan. He stepped quietly next to her. As he did, he slid on a pair of latex gloves. With a finger over his mouth, he signaled her to be quiet. Then he pointed to the door for her to leave. The therapist didn't argue. She exited the room quickly. Juan took over where the therapist had been massaging Monty. His groaning continued.

It was now four o'clock and Juan hoped that he could buy a little time for Ray. He continued to massage the lunatic's back and softened up his touch when Monty squirmed.

"Ouch! Not so hard." Monty glanced at his watch. "I need to get going. I'm late for a meeting."

In a voice that sounded like Julia Child, Juan began his treatment. "Now, now, Mr. Handsome, aren't you the boss? Who cares if you're a little late? It's time for Ruby's famous facial. It will make this handsome devil even handsomer. I might have to take you home myself."

Monty turned himself over as he tried to get up. Upon seeing the big woman that looked like a retired hooker, he blurted, "Oooh, gaawwd!" in disgust. "Where's the other woman?" Monty was about to say something else when Juan pushed him back down on the table. He reached for one of the steaming towels on the hot towel rack and slapped it on Monty's face. He wrapped it tightly. Monty's arms and legs flailed as he convulsed to free himself. Juan held on tightly as the table started to roll.

"Oh my, you're a strong one. I like that in a man." Juan held the towel firmly against Monty's face. "Oh, come now, a little warm is it? That's the way we like it, so our pores open up and are allowed to breathe." Juan continued his rant and removed the towel.

Monty started to sit up and say something, but he felt the heavy woman's hand flatten him on the table again. Juan took a gob of cream and slapped it on Monty's face and smeared it thoroughly. Monty was trying to say something, but when he opened his mouth, it got filled with cream. Juan then slapped a cucumber slice on each eye. He was still pinning Monty against the table.

"There now, I want you to relax and become one with the cucumber. You must be the essence of cucumber. That is the secret to taking years off your face. It has worked for me, and it can work for you."

Monty managed to free his arm and flung the cucumbers off his face. They flew across the room and stuck to the wall with a splat. They hung there like a pair of eyes. The wallpaper in the room had a pattern of wiggly lines. The cucumbers and wallpaper's wiggly lines combined to make a not-so-happy face.

Monty, freed at last from the ugly woman's grip, barked: "Now listen, you witch, you'd better clean me up so I can get out of here, and I mean NOW!"

"Oh you're a testy one. Very well, Mr. Impatience." Juan took a towel and wiped Monty's face. "Say, aren't you a handsome devil. You look ten years younger."

Monty reached for the hand-mirror and looked at himself. "I do?"

Then Juan tried to continue buying more time for Ray by reaching for a Q-tip. "Here, let me take another five years off you with my secret pressure point facial massage." He started poking at Monty's cheeks and his forehead with Q-tips. Before Monty realized what was happening, he felt the other hand of monster woman trying to lay him back down.

Monty shoved Juan's hands to the side and exploded. "Get away from me, you behemoth! Now get out of here and let me get dressed."

"Shy, are you? Oh, I like that in a man."

"Get out, NOW!"

Juan left the room and approached the ladies at the counter. "He's a cranky one, can't say that I blame him. His Longfellow is itsy bitsy." Juan held up his thumb and index finger motioning one inch apart. He left Vivian's and ran across to his drugstore post and texted Ray.

"He's on his way!"

It was now ten minutes past four and Ray still had not found anything. Juan watched Monty exit the building. Ray had not responded. Juan decided to call him. Ray picked up the phone. "I stalled him as long as possible. He's on his way. He'll be there any minute."

Ray answered right away. "I've got to keep looking – meet

me in the car later. I'm parked in the office parking lot, level 1, close to the elevators."

As Ray put the phone back into his pocket, he spotted what looked like a small statue on the book shelf. He wondered if it could be a small lamp. He didn't pay any attention to it before because he was looking for a regular lamp. It was small and was the only decorative object on the beautiful cherry wood bookcase. Ray walked over and examined it. There were three little holes on the top of it. "Could this be it?"

Monty stepped off the elevator and marched toward his office. He did not say anything to Peggy. She tried to get his attention. "Your four o'clock appointment is waiting in your office."

He ignored her and walked quickly past her. He opened the door to his office and found Ray standing over his desk. "What are you doing?" he demanded.

Ray looked up and smiled. "Hello, Mr. McPride. I was just spreading this paperwork out on your desk for your convenience. It contains the latest results for the BD109 bonding agent."

Monty gave Ray a cautious looking over, then slowly stepped toward the desk. "Oh, yes, of course, and how are we doing?"

"We have fixed the formulation, and it is on spec, Mr. McPride."

Monty sat down in his chair, now a little more relaxed that he was getting the news he wanted to hear. "And when will we be ready for mass production?"

"Once we submit the test results and appropriate paperwork, it should be ready for mass production in two months."

Monty looked slightly annoyed. "That's fine. How about limited test production? Can we do that now with all the test results in?"

Ray thought for a moment. "You're probably looking at three weeks for limited test production approval."

Monty waved his hand. "I don't know why everything takes so long, but no matter. Do you have my sample of the formulation as I requested at our previous meeting?"

"A sample?"

Monty stood up and peered at Ray. "Yes, Mr. Cromwell,

don't play stupid with me. I meant every word I said. Now, hand over the BD109 or I will fire you and your company from this account effective immediately."

Ray was unsure how to respond because he really did not have a sample vial of BD109. He had forgotten to request one from KC to bring to the meeting. He was sure that Monty would fire him anyway.

Ray began to explain, "But, Mr. McPride, I for…"

Monty slammed his hand on his desk and yelled. "Mr. Cromwell, this is your last chance. Hand over what you have in that briefcase of yours or I will call security to escort you out, and your business with us will be finished."

Monty's phone buzzed. It was Peggy. "Not now, Peggy. I'm in a meeting."

"Sorry to bother you, Mr. McPride, but we have a situation in the lobby. It seems that Mr. Diaz, one the men you fired, is downstairs. Security has apprehended him. He had a gun. It turned out to be a toy gun, but they want to speak to someone about pressing charges."

"I'll be down as soon as I can. If they can't wait, then they can figure out what to do with him. I really don't care."

"OK, Mr. McPride, I'll have them wait for you."

While Monty was on the phone, Ray dug through his briefcase, hoping that he might have another vial of BD109. He opened every flap of his briefcase and then stopped when he saw the little vial of green food coloring that had somehow made its way into his briefcase. When Monty got off the phone, he walked over to Ray and extended his hand.

"Hand it over, Mr. Cromwell. This is the last time I am goint to ask."

Ray took the small vial of green food coloring and placed it in Monty's hand.

Monty smiled. "There, that wasn't so hard was it, Mr. Cromwell? I have a good mind to fire you anyway, but I don't want to waste time with the paperwork transfer to a new lab. Mind you, Mr. Cromwell, do not cross me. I can be your best friend or your worst enemy. Now, please, pick up your papers and call me when you have limited production approval."

Monty did not wait for Ray to leave the office. He was

about to pick up the phone and dial Wilkins when his phone rang.

"Yes? I have it...I see. Very well, I'll meet you in your office."

Monty walked to the door with the vial in hand. "Good day, Mr. Cromwell." He stood by the door waiting for Ray to gather his things and get out. Ray hurried up and left. Monty closed the door and proceeded to Wilkins' office.

Wilkins was waiting at his desk when Monty entered holding the vial. "Here it is. Call Rogers and have him come pick it up and start production. We can give out samples to our prospective customers. We'll have druggies clamoring for this stuff after they've sampled it. We can start replicating this in our little lab tonight. Hurry it up. I'll meet you downstairs so we can take care of our other little situation."

Ray approached his car. Juan was leaning against it. "Why are you wearing lipstick?"

Juan wiped the remaining lipstick off his face. "I was trying to stall him." The wig was bundled up and in his pocket.

Ray laughed. "I won't ask."

"Did you find the recorder?"

Ray gave him a nod. "I think so, but I don't want to examine it here. Let's get out of here first." They climbed into the car and headed out. They approached the parking attendant. Ray handed him the time ticket.

The attendant took it. "Thank you, just a moment."

Ray's phone buzzed. It was a text from Peggy.

"Did u find anything?"

Before Ray had a chance to reply to the text message, the rear passenger doors opened as Monty and Wilkins both got in the car.

The parking attendant was nowhere to be seen. Wilkins pressed a button on his phone and the gate opened.

"Drive on, ladies," Monty instructed as he pointed a gun equipped with a silencer at the back of Ray's head. Ray froze as he felt the gun dig into the back of his head. "I said drive on," Monty repeated with clenched teeth. Ray slowly drove out of the parking garage and turned to go with the flow of the one-way traffic.

Ray and Juan looked at each other in disbelief.

"You can thank Wilkins here. He's my little techno-elf. Mr. Cromwell, did I not tell you that I know everything that goes on in my office, not to mention, everything that my receptionist says or types into that cell phone of hers? The information doesn't get to me instantaneously, but it eventually gets to me. The question is: What am I going to do with you two idiots? Oh, and Mr. Cromwell, please hand over the salt shaker that you took from my office."

"Salt shaker?"

"Yes, Mr. Cromwell, a salt shaker." Monty made a pouty face. "Oh poor rittle Ray thought it was a secret recorder. Oh, poor, poor, boy." Monty laughed. "You two are such fools. I had Wilkins remove that little item this very afternoon."

Juan turned to look at Monty. "You won't get away with it."

Monty then looked over at Juan. "I always get away with it. There is nothing you can do to stop me, loser." Then he examined Juan more closely. "Say, I know you. You look like that loser that was in my class way back when." Then he studied Juan again and laughed. "Well, isn't this a fine class reunion, and what's with the costume?"

"I like to dress up."

Wilkins chimed in, "I think this is the guy with the weird medical condition. I read something about it. He has to wear it due to some kind of freak accident."

Monty was very interested in this bit of news. "What's the medical condition?"

Wilkins continued. "He has to wear it, or he dies in five minutes, something about his body's electrical signals. I subscribe to a freak news blog, and it showed up as a story."

Monty laughed. "You expect me to believe this?"

"It's true, Mr. McPride," replied Wilkins. "Weird but true. He's some kind of medical freak."

Monty laughed again. "No way! This is fabulous! It would be too easy." Then Monty got an idea. They drove for another five minutes. "Pull into that alley." He nudged the back of Ray's head with the gun.

It had started to rain and the sky was getting dark. As Ray pulled into the alley, he suddenly stepped hard on the brake. They all lunged forward and he made a grab for the gun in Monty's hand. Monty pulled back and hit Ray on the head with the butt of the gun. A trickle of blood oozed from the wound.

"Try that again and I won't hesitate to blow your brains out."

He handed Wilkins a second gun. "All right, Wilkins, let's test your theory."

Then he signaled to Juan. "Now, get out of the car, loser and stand over there." Monty looked over at Wilkins. "I want you to cover him." Then he turned to Juan with his signature sick Monty sneer. "Now, take off the stupid rabbit costume."

Juan pleaded, "Please, I can't, I really..."

"Shut up and take it off or I'll waste you right here. Take your pick." Monty was enjoying this tremendously.

Juan slowly undid the costume and stepped out of it.

"Now give it to me," Monty demanded. Wilkins picked it up and threw it in the back seat.

Then Monty instructed Wilkins, "Stay with him here. If he's still alive after five minutes, kill him."

He looked at Ray in the rear view mirror. "You will drive me to the nursing home. Me and the old man have some unfinished business."

Wilkins was starting to look a little frazzled. "Mr. McPride, I don't know about this. I don't think I can. Why don't we just..."

Monty roared, "Don't wimp out on me now, Wilkins. You've come too far and are in this too deep. Besides, you want that promotion, don't you? I'll see you in the morning. We'll talk about it after the staff meeting. Everything will be as it should be after tonight. No more loose ends. And, if what you say is true, you won't have to kill him, just let him die. Talk about convenient!"

Monty nudged Ray's throbbing head. "Drive on. It's time to go see daddy."

Ray reluctantly drove off, feeling powerless to save his brother-in-law.

Wilkins stood beneath a small overhang in the dark, rain-drenched evening. He looked at the man shivering in front of him. "I didn't bargain for this, but it's got to get done." It was two minutes since Juan had taken off the rabbit costume. He still felt OK. Wilkins looked at his watch. "I hope what I read about you is true. I'd hate to have to shoot you."

"Why don't you just get me to a hospital while there's still time? Do you really want to be an accessory to murder?" Juan dropped to one knee. He was starting to feel lightheaded. He got up and recovered his balance.

"I can't."

Juan pleaded. "You don't have to do this, you know. Please, there might still be time to get me to a hospital." Juan felt increasingly lightheaded and he dropped down to both knees. He looked at Wilkins and struggled to get up. The rain was falling harder now. It was almost dark. The evening was starting to get cold and the wind was picking up.

"It's what Mr. McPride wants."

Juan was now holding onto the wall behind him for balance. He was slowly swaying from side to side.

"And what do you want, Wilkins? You have everything to lose and nothing to gain by what you are doing." Juan was now sliding against the wall, sliding down to the ground as he clutched at the wall for stability.

Wilkins continued pointing the gun at Juan, although by now it was becoming apparent that he would not need to use it. "I'm going to be a very wealthy man."

Juan struggled to pull himself to an upright position and scraped his hands on the rough brick wall. His eyes were getting blurry. He was barely able to stand. He stood motionless for a moment, like a man frozen in time. Then he looked at Wilkins. "Please, help me." His words were slurred. Juan's eyes were closing. He extended his right arm and opened his hand as though he wanted to grab Wilkins, and uttered, "I forgive you." He fell in slow motion onto the pavement with puddles of rain all around him.

Wilkins stood there for a moment, still holding the eerie image of Juan standing there with his hand extended. He looked like a ghost. It spooked Wilkins enough that he took several steps back as Juan held his hand out. He waited another moment; there was no movement. Then he walked up and kicked the body in the ribs to make sure he was dead. There was still no movement.

Wilkins bent down to take Juan's pulse, but there was no pulse. Now that his assignment was completed, he looked around. All was quiet. He walked casually out of the alley and into the street. He walked a few blocks to a busy intersection and hailed a cab.

Monty and Ray arrived at the nursing home. He told Ray to park in a secluded part of the parking lot. He threw a pair of handcuffs into Ray's lap. "Here, put these on, but first, hit the trunk release. If you try anything, I'll waste you right here. It doesn't really matter to me."

Ray put on the handcuffs. Then Monty gagged him.

"Now, get out of the car slowly and get in the trunk."

Ray knew he was going to die and couldn't stop thinking of Juan, who was probably dead by now. He got into the trunk, and Monty bound his feet tightly with rope. Then it went completely dark as the trunk lid slammed shut and clicked when Monty locked it.

Ray thought of Angie and the boys and how he would never see them again. There was no way this lunatic was going to let him live. He heard Monty walking away and tried furiously to free himself and kick the trunk lid open, but the trunk did not budge.

Monty approached the back entrance of the nursing home. It was quiet, dark and dreary outside. The rain did a good job of masking any noise. He noticed a young woman outside the rear of the building. She was standing under a small canopy, next to a storage shed. She was smoking a cigarette and talking on her cell phone. Her back was turned to him, oblivious that he was upon her. He put the gun to the back of her head and took the phone from her hands. He calmly hit the "end" button to terminate her call.

"If you turn around and look at me, you die," he said in a calm and determined voice. "Give me your keys." She handed him her electronic key card. "Now, listen very carefully."

The young woman nodded without hesitation.

He pressed the gun to her head. "You're going to crawl into that storage shed and maybe I won't blow your brains out. Then I will lock you inside, and you will remain quiet for thirty minutes. I hope that you're a good slow counter because if I hear anything before that, I'll kill you. After thirty-minutes, you can scream till the cows come home. You got that?"

She nodded and unlocked the storage shed door with a regular key. He snatched it from her when she had finished. Then she obediently walked inside. He locked it and headed to the nursing home's rear door.

Juan lay drenched on the puddled ground. The rain was still coming down. There was the distant sound of an occasional vehicle driving on the wet roads. A few moments later the rain stopped all together. All you could hear were the trickles of drops as they ran off and landed in puddles. It was a quiet symphony of droplets which was soon accompanied by a gentle scraping sound. The sound got a bit louder as the wind blew the chilly night air. Someone was approaching. The steps grew louder as the person came closer. A pair of black sandaled feet stopped when they reached Juan's body.

The stranger bent down and covered Juan in a white blanket. Then he gently placed his hands under Juan's body and lifted him into his arms. "Come on, son. Let's get you out of here." It was a familiar voice.

Monty entered the building and had no trouble avoiding the few workers who were on shift. He headed to Blake McPride's room. Peggy had given him the room number earlier. He heard voices approaching, so he stood still until they passed. They were headed down the other corridor that formed the top of the T-shaped building. He came to Room 158. The little sign outside the room was labeled "Blake McPride."

Monty paused to listen. If someone happened to be with the old geezer, he would have to do them both. He could not afford to leave the old man alive. He had been careless not to finish him off sooner. He listened closely. There was no sound inside the room. He hoped that the old man was not being given a bath or something. That would be most inconvenient. He quietly grasped the door handle and gently opened it. The dimly lit room revealed the bed, but it was empty. Then Monty stepped in further and saw Blake McPride sitting in his recliner.

Monty had always been lucky. It seemed like the devil

would be dancing tonight. He pulled his gun up to finish the old man once and for all. Then he felt a chill and the hairs on the back of his neck got cold. He got an intense case of goose bumps as he felt the cold hard barrel of a gun being pressed against the side of his neck, just below his left ear.

"Drop it," the voice from behind instructed, "Nice and easy, and kick it away from you."

Monty paused, reluctant to comply. "I wouldn't think that hard about it, my finger is apt to tense up real quick," the voice said.

Monty put the gun on the floor and gently kicked it away. Then he turned his head a little, as though trying to look around the corner, to see who had the gun to his head.

There was a rustling sound directly in front of him, and as he turned forward again, Monty squealed like a school girl when he saw Blake McPride standing in front of him. In one hand, Blake held the gun that Monty had put on the floor. In the other, he held a chocolate bar of which he casually took a small bite. "Hello, Monty."

Monty was clammy with sweat and turned pale as though someone suddenly applied bad zombie make-up on him. He tried to speak but only fragments of words came out of his suddenly dry throat.

"What? How?" He gulped, trying to get rid of the sandy taste in his throat. "It's good to see you, Dad," Monty blurted, trying to get his composure but sounding like a bad actor who had forgotten his lines. "This is a strange but pleasant surprise."

Blake smiled. "Yes, strange indeed. A miracle you might say." He looked at the chocolate bar. "The miracle of chocolate!" Then he took another small bite.

Monty made a sad face and broke down. "I don't know what got into me, Dad. Can you forgive me? I promise I will make it up to you. I was a fool. I realize that now. Thank God you're OK after the terrible thing I did."

Blake looked at Monty as a thoughtful, caring father might look at his little boy who had made an honest mistake. "Sure, son, sure... I'd forgive you if I thought you really wanted forgiveness." Then Blake's eyes widened. "It's amazing how fast some folks can find the goodness in their hearts and find religion with a loaded gun pressed to the back of their head. Can I get an Amen, Monty? Where are my manners, let me introduce you to my friends Officers McNally and Hernandez, meet Monty."

Then he looked at Monty with daggers in his eyes. "Yes, you are a fool, and you are my son, and you're going to jail. Boys, please arrest my idiot son."

Monty bolted just as both officers were about to arrest him. With his arms flying wildly, he ran out of the room and down the corridor toward the front door. The two officers ran out of the room in pursuit. Monty ran like a track star. He was putting a good amount of distance between himself and the officers. He ran out through the front doors and headed down the street. As the police came out of the building, they paused to see in which direction he had run. They spotted him running like the wind toward the corner, his hair flying, his extended eyelashes now pressed up against his eyebrows, and his new suit blowing in the wind as he ran like a wild man.

He jumped over a trash can in his path and continued his amazing sprint. The officers looked at each other. Hernandez yelled to McNally, "He's too fast. We're not going to catch him on foot."

Monty hurdled and cleared several obstacles in his path. It was as if his feet had sprouted wings. He cleared another hurdle and landed in the street just in time to hear the blast from the truck's horn. The officers, who had started slowing down, heard the horn blast followed by the agonizing screech of locking brake wheels, immediately followed by several loud thuds.

As the officers arrived at the accident scene, the driver climbed down from the truck. "He just came out of nowhere. I didn't have time to stop."

Hernandez and McNally got busy making their report. Monty was killed on impact. No charges would be filed against the driver.

Another vehicle pulled up beside the two officers. Inside was undercover officer Kate Dentin, who had posed as one of the employees and had been put in the storage shed. She rolled down her window. Ray Cromwell was in the rear passenger seat.

"Well, Hernandez, it looks like you got him."

Hernandez pointed to the truck. "You can thank the bug

truck for this little bit of justice." She looked at the Mantis Moving Company truck with the large praying mantis logo on the side.

"We're going to check on the other victim," said Officer Dentin. "I called an ambulance. They should be on their way to the location. His friend thinks it may be too late. I'll see you later."

They sped off to the alley.

27

The Little Red House

Juan woke up and saw the somewhat familiar face of the man sitting across from him.

"What happened?"

"You had a close call, son. You stopped breathing for a while."

Juan started to panic and get up. "I need to run. We need to call the police. Blake McPride is in danger. So is Ray!"

The man gently touched Juan's shoulder, signaling him to stay put. "Relax, son. The old man is safe."

"How do you know?"

"I just know." The man's voice was calm.

"But Monty's going to get away with murder!"

"Son, nobody gets away with anything. Monty is getting what he deserves, trust me."

"I hope you're right."

"Always," the man replied.

Juan looked at the black gentleman closely. "You look familiar. Do I know you?"

The man smiled. "You should. We shared a meal together a few days ago."

Juan was surprised and embarrassed at the same time. "You're the guy from the mall! Hey, I'm sorry about that. I thought you had..."

The man waved his hand "Don't worry about it, Juan. I

enjoyed sharing my meal with you."

Juan studied the man's face for a moment. "You look like the guy that saved Monty's life that time at school. Was that you?"

The man nodded.

Juan did the math in his head. *"How can it be? That was twenty-five years ago."* He looked around at the modest surroundings. "How did I get here?"

"I carried you."

"Alone?"

"I'm in pretty good shape for an old guy."

"Where am I?"

"You're in my house."

"How come I'm not dead? I was forced out of the rabbit costume that was keeping me alive."

"It appears you won't be needing it anymore."

Juan was confused. "I don't understand."

The man gave a smile. "You don't need to, son." He paused for a moment. "How are you feeling, Juan?"

Juan thought carefully about how he was actually feeling. "A little disoriented at first, but I feel OK... No, come to think of it, I feel excellent!" He took a deep breath. "Wow, I don't think I've ever felt this good."

The man smiled. "Well, that's good. You'd better get going and let your friends know you're OK. There are some clothes in the other room that should fit you, and help yourself to a snack."

"Yeah, I'd better get going." Juan was still taking it all in. He wondered if he could really be free of the rabbit costume. He turned to the man. "Thank you for saving me."

"You're welcome. It's what I do." Then the man stood up. "Now that we know each other, don't be a stranger. Come back and visit. OK?" The man looked at Juan, still wearing that little smile. Juan liked the man's smile. There was something about it that made him feel good.

Juan smiled back. "I think I will." Then he went into the other room and tried on a pair of pants, a shirt and a pair of sneakers. "These clothes, they fit just right! Thank you again!" He came out of the room, but the man was gone.

Juan helped himself to a snack and left. He looked back at the little red house and noticed the street sign that read "Leesville

Road." He wanted to come back again to bring the nice man a gift for saving his life. Juan walked toward the highway and across the overpass toward town.

The ambulance arrived at the designated scene and reported that there was no body lying in the alley. The unmarked police car with officer Dentin and Ray arrived a few minutes later.

"Is this the location?" asked Officer Dentin.

Ray got out and looked at the alleyway. "Yes, I'm sure this is where he got out."

"Maybe another police car found the dead body." Officer Dentin reached for the walkie-talkie and asked if anyone had reported finding a body in the vicinity of the alley.

"Negative," came the reply.

"Well, Mr. Cromwell, I'll drop you off at your house if you'd like, and we'll call you if he turns up."

Ray was numb as he got back into the car. They drove off. He couldn't help feeling guilty that he did not do more to try and save Juan. He gazed hypnotically out the window as they passed houses and parked cars. Ray closed his eyes and replayed the events that had taken place. Then the patrol car hit a pothole and Ray snapped out of his trance. A few seconds later he yelled, "Stop the car!"

Officer Dentin looked at him. "What's the matter, Mr. Cromwell? Are you all right?"

Ray pointed backwards. He opened the car door and ran to catch up with the man they had just passed. The lonely figure walking on the side of the road looked like Juan and he was carrying a pack of yellow peeps.

Juan saw a man running toward him.

Ray yelled, "Juan, is that you?" He was now close enough to see that it really was Juan. He was alive and walking, wearing plain clothes. He almost didn't recognize him without the rabbit costume.

He hugged his brother-in-law as tears rolled down his face. "Man, I thought you were dead. I felt terrible leaving you back there, knowing you were going to die. Is it really you? I can't believe it." Ray grabbed Juan's face with both hands and looked into his eyes. "It is you! Thank God!"

The unmarked car pulled up alongside the two men. "Is this the man you thought was dead?" asked Officer Dentin.

"Yes," Ray replied. "I thought we'd lost him."

"Well, looks like he's been found. C'mon, both of you get in." They got into the vehicle wiping away their tears.

Ray asked Officer Dentin if she could drop them off at the nursing home. She agreed. Then he turned to Juan. "Where did you get the Peeps?"

Linda looked up at the men standing in the doorway to her office. She jumped out of her chair and ran over to give Juan a hug. "Juan, I'm so glad you're safe. I thought you were dead!"

"So did I, what happened?" Juan enjoyed the hug. "Is the old man OK?"

"Mr. McPride, Sr., is fine. He was discharged not too long ago. It's really weird. One minute, he was sitting there, barely able to move. The next, he was standing up like nothing was ever wrong with him. He assured me that he felt fine and asked me to call the police. He told me how much he appreciated your one-sided conversations with him. Although he was paralyzed, his hearing was not impaired.

When the police arrived, they set people up all around the building, and they had Officer Dentin act as a decoy. She was never in any real danger. I had Dr. Kildare, one of the staff doctors, examine Blake before we sent him home, and he appeared to be in perfect health. He doesn't seem to need his heart medicine anymore. He's going to see the specialist next week, just to make sure nothing is wrong."

Juan raised his eyebrows, "You mean it was a miracle?"

"Well, I don't know about that," Linda said. "Dr. Kildare observed that the blood test revealed elevated amounts of cocoa. He thinks that this particular cocoa contained unusual properties, which may have somehow triggered a chemical reaction in his system and…"

Ray interrupted with a laugh. "You mean the man was cured by chocolate?"

Juan and Linda looked at each other and chuckled at such a crazy idea.

"Well, I guess you can thank your son for that," Juan said

as he looked at Linda. "Whenever I came to Blake's room, I'd share a little bit of chocolate that I got from Ben. The desserts here are so blah."

She smiled. "You know, you weren't supposed to do that." Then she stepped back for a moment and looked at Juan from top to bottom. "You're not in your rabbit costume. How is that possible? I thought you couldn't survive without it?"

"It's a long story, Linda. I guess you could say I'm a new man."

Diogenes Ruiz

28

The Reunion

The board of directors and department heads filled the large conference room for the emergency meeting. Peggy sat wondering what idiotic tasks Monty might have for her to do today. She dreaded coming to work more and more each day. There were a growing number of items that needed to be addressed, and he had yet to respond to the many requests from department heads.

"Where is he?" asked Fred Lindsay, one of the departmental heads.

"I don't know," Peggy replied. "Perhaps Wilkins might know. He's been spending a lot of time with Monty lately." Wilkins sat in his usual seat. He seemed unconcerned while playing some game on his phone as everyone waited for Monty.

Pete Harris, another department head, leaned toward Peggy. "He's probably getting his nails done or having a spa treatment."

Peggy turned to Pete. "This company is in real trouble, Pete. I think everybody knows it."

Suddenly, there was noise coming from outside the conference room as people started to cheer. Then the conference room doors opened and Blake McPride entered the room. Everyone spontaneously rose to their feet and broke into applause. Mr. McPride proceeded to the head of the table and took his seat.

Everyone was still standing and applauding. He motioned to them, "Please, sit down."

Fred Lyndsay remained standing and said what everybody

in the room was feeling. "Mr. McPride, on behalf of the board of directors and the staff, I think I speak for everyone when I say that we are delighted to see you back."

Everyone broke into applause again and nodded in agreement.

Peggy turned to him. "Where is Monty?"

"Monty has gone to meet his maker, Peggy." The room became completely quiet. He paused for a moment. "My poor misguided son was killed in an accident last night as he tried to elude the police. I only hope that God has mercy on the both of us." Then Blake McPride looked up. "Now, dear friends, let's get back to business. Oh, but before we begin..." Blake paused to glance at Wilkins who was sitting very low in his seat. He seemed to be fidgeting as all eyes turned to him. He was shiny with sweat. After looking at Wilkins for a long suspense-filled moment, Wilkins finally looked at Blake. "Wilkins, you little maggot, you're fired!"

Two security men walked in on cue.

"Please escort Mr. Wilkins to his new home at the police station, where he will be booked for embezzlement, fraud, kidnapping and attempted murder."

Wilkins was escorted out of the conference room.

"There's one more piece of unfinished business," he said to the group. Then Blake McPride called to have Ray Cromwell brought into the conference room. All eyes turned as Ray entered.

"Mr. Cromwell, I would personally like to thank you and your brother-in-law for all you did to try and stop my misguided son. You have been a loyal and hardworking part of our team. I would like you to head up our new BD109 division. I think this new product can do a lot of good, with good people leading the way."

Everyone in the room applauded. Then Blake asked, "Ray, do you think Juan would like to join our creative department? We need a good photographer, and Ms. Linda tells me that he's very good."

Ray smiled. "I can't speak for him, but my guess is that he would be delighted, sir!"

Blake turned to Peggy. "Get Juan in here this week and let's get the show on the road." Peggy nodded. He continued. "I'm going to be very busy next week undoing some of the damage that Monty caused, starting with rehiring Diaz, Jacobs and Ramirez and presenting the sales award to its proper recipient. Have Juan join me for lunch. In fact, I understand my old friend Harold Jones will be in town next week. Why don't you have Juan join Harold and me for lunch? It would make better use of my time. Harold is a photographer for that magazine. What's the name of it?"

"*National Geographic*," Peggy added.

"Yes, that's the one."

"Yes, sir, I'll take care of it."

Blake then looked around the room. "Where's Delmont?"

"John's out of town," Peggy explained. "His sister took ill last week with appendicitis and was rushed to the emergency room. She is now recovering. He took the red eye out at around 2:00 am a few nights ago to be with her. He should be back in a couple of days. Unfortunately, his apartment burned down while he was away, but no one was hurt."

"That's too bad about his place. I'm glad his sister is all right." Then Blake McPride turned his attention to the group.

"Now, my dear friends and colleagues, let's get back to business."

29

Looking for Answers

It was a gorgeous spring day. Plants were bursting with the rich colors of new life. It had been five weeks since Blake McPride and Juan Arias both experienced miraculous recoveries. Juan and Linda were on their way to a church which had been recommended by a friend. They wanted to make arrangements for their wedding. Their relationship had blossomed quickly, and they both felt the time was right to enter into matrimony. Juan's previous marriage to Leigh had taken place at a justice-of-the-peace when they spent the weekend in Las Vegas. This time Juan wanted to do it differently.

As they turned into the parking lot of St. Ignatius on Leesville Road, Juan looked intently at the church building. "This can't be right. There's a church here, but there is supposed to be a house right here, a little red house. I saw it. I walked into the other room and got clothes to wear just a few weeks ago. I remember leaving the house and walking down Leesville Road across the interstate overpass. Shortly after that, I saw Ray running toward me. I know it was right here."

They entered the church office to meet with Fr. Ken, one of the priests at the parish. Fr. Ken greeted them, and they sat in his office.

Juan looked at the items hanging in Fr. Ken's office for anything that might show the date the parish was started. "Excuse me, Father. How long has this church been here?"

"Thirty years, Mr. Arias. Why do you ask?"

Juan looked a little puzzled. "Well, I could have sworn there was a little house where this church is now. It was a little red house."

Fr. Ken smiled. "Why, yes, there was a small red house on this property. It was where the church began. It was moved to another town when we outgrew it. We needed to make room for the larger church."

Juan thought for a moment. "That can't be. See, I was here, I mean there, in the little red house, just a few weeks ago."

I guess you can say that there is a house on this property, Mr. Arias. It's not a little red house, but it is a house of God. Then Father Ken handed Juan a magazine. It had been recently printed to commemorate the parish's thirty year anniversary. He opened to a page and pointed to one of the pictures. "Is that the house you saw?"

Juan stared at the picture for a moment and then looked up at Father Ken. "That's it!"

Fr. Ken smiled. "Did you have a little too much wine that evening?"

Juan laughed. "No, I wasn't drunk. I was there. Someone saved my life that night, and he took me there. He said he lived here, I mean there."

Fr. Ken leaned forward and signaled Juan to do the same as though he wanted to share a little secret. Then he whispered. "And so He does."

Juan sat back in the chair thinking about his experience. Father Ken looked at Linda and joked, "If you think he's crazy, you don't have to marry him you know."

She laughed. "He's a little crazy, but in a good sort of way."

Juan pointed to a photo on Fr. Ken's wall. How many priests do you have here? Is that a picture of them?

Fr. Ken turned and looked at the photo. "Yes, we have three priests. We are two at the moment. That's me on the left. Pastor Bob is in the middle. Fr. Oliver is on the right. He is an interesting man. He's on extended leave at the moment."

"OK, Father, I'm sorry. I don't mean to take up a lot of

your time. We want to get married here at St. Ignatius. I get the feeling that this is where we belong."

Fr. Ken smiled. "Very well, here's what I we need the two of you to do."

Juan looked apologetically at Fr. Ken as he interrupted him one more time. "Father, I'm sorry, but I have one last question before we go on, and I promise not to interrupt you again." He paused. "Do you have a black priest here who looks like Morgan Freeman?"

Diogenes Ruiz

30

Two Years Later

Juan, Linda, Ben and six month old Sophie entered the vestibule of St. Ignatius Church. They greeted a few friends and then went into the worship space. They sat near the back just in case little Sophie needed to be taken outside for a diaper change or a cry.

Linda turned to Juan. "Honey, can you go to the car and get me Sophie's bag? I can't believe we left it in the car."

Juan hurried to the car and found the bag. He ran across the parking lot and noticed a man whom he thought he recognized. He seemed to be a landscape maintenance person. As the man turned, Juan stopped.

"It's you!" Juan was delighted and surprised to see him.

"Hi, Juan."

"What are you doing here?"

"Delivering good news." The man's smile seemed to brighten an already sunny day.

Juan grinned. "What good news? Who are you, really?" Then Juan looked closely into the man's eyes and said, "Are you...?"

"I AM," the man replied before Juan could say another word.

Juan's grin was now a full-fledged smile. "You show up at the most unexpected times."

"I'm always here, Juan, everywhere. Just look into their

eyes."

Then the man smiled and asked, "So, how's your job at National Geographic? Are you happy, Juan?"

Juan's face beamed. "Oh yeah, couldn't be better. I love my work. It's what I always dreamed of when I was a kid."

The man seemed pleased. "Hmm, yeah. Love is good." Then he looked up at the blue sky and back down to Juan. "Well, enjoy this beautiful Easter Sunday, Juan, and enjoy your three wonderful children."

Juan's eyebrows seemed to want to pop off his head. "We don't have three children."

The man gave a wink. "Not yet."

The music started, and Juan glanced at the entrance of the church. The Easter Mass was beginning. He looked back at the man, but the man was gone.

Juan walked back into the church, sat down next to Ben and Sophie. Then he leaned over and looked into his wife's eyes. In those eyes, he saw love looking back. He felt the presence of God stirring in his heart, like the powerful swell of an ocean's wave, only this was no ordinary wave. It seemed to have no crest. With an overwhelming feeling of love and abundance, he felt as though he would explode if he moved. He felt tears of grateful joy pooling in his eyes. He was still and present in that moment. *"How could I be so loved?"* Juan thought. *"I have done nothing to deserve this."* Heaven came to earth in that instant as he surrendered to God's unconditional love and grace.

The priest began Mass and Juan and Linda slowly turned to look at the altar. They wiped their eyes and sat down to hear the good news. On this Easter Sunday, they would hear the story of a loving God who sacrificed His only begotten son. Fr. Ken would tell the story of how Jesus was crucified for our sake and how, on the third day after His death, He rose to conquer death so that our mortal chains could be broken forever.

Juan sat silently in church on that Easter Sunday and thought of the remarkable gift of renewal that he had received. As he listened to Fr. Ken's homily, he bowed his head and felt his heart swell with gratitude. Juan looked at the figure on the cross, above the altar and simply gave thanks.

Epilogue

Like a worn, discarded rabbit costume, our old lives can be renewed through Christ. We do not need to cling to the past or to our deficiencies. That is not what defines us in the eyes of God. Easter is the celebration of that renewal that happens through Christ. We can shut Him out, or accept His invitation to love in a spirit of gratitude and humility. Our free will is completely our own, but through Him, it is Divine. We are the manifestation of Christ for one another. Heaven is made by each of us, in the smallest gestures of kindness and love. Free will is the gatekeeper.

The invitation is there for anyone who chooses to accept it.

Thank you for reading *A Rabbit's Tale, An Easter Story*. Please take a few minutes to write a review and post it on Amazon. In the world of self-published books, reviews rule and I am hoping that folks who enjoy the book will help me spread the news.

If you hated the book, please accept my sincere thanks for taking the time to read it. I realize that there are a gazillion books out there and you chose to read mine. I am truly grateful.

Diogenes Ruiz

Connecting More of the Dots

The woman who thanked Juan for getting her morning started with a laugh had been suffering from a deep depression. She had prayed for guidance. She needed to feel that things would be OK. When she saw Juan and everybody laughed at him in the elevator, it was a sign to her that she could be OK. She thanked God for the little blessing and started to apply herself to think positively about what she could change, instead of focusing on things that she could not.

When the police pulled Juan over for the second time, it saved his life. Had he kept driving, he would have been hit broadside by the man speeding trying to make the yellow light. Juan would have been killed.

When Juan sat down with the stranger by mistake, thinking that his food had been stolen, he forgot about Leigh and Bill sitting across the food court. It avoided him having a confrontation with Bill and getting into a nasty brawl. He would have been arrested, and Bill would have pressed charges. Juan would have spent time in jail and would have had more financial complications as a result of that encounter. Fortunately, he was preoccupied.

A couple of years later, Juan received a letter from Fred Wilkins. It was from the prison where Wilkins was serving his eight-year sentence. While serving his prison time, Fred had plenty of time to reflect on what he had done. He started to read the Bible and eventually became a follower of Christ. In his letter to Juan, he asked for forgiveness for what he had done. Juan visited Fred and brought a few chocolate bars to him. Upon his release, Fred moved to Cleveland to be closer to family. He found work as a janitor and eventually got hired by a small computer company. He prayed for Juan and his family often.

Questions to Consider

What does the rabbit costume represent?

How has Christ been present in your life at times when you may not have recognized Him?

Can you remember times when God might have invited you to be Christ for others?

Is there something preventing you from having a deeper relationship with Christ?

What mud has Jesus rubbed in your eyes?

How has the risen Jesus been present in our everyday lives?

How have you been changed by what happened on Easter?

What are some things you can do to be drawn closer to Jesus?

For Those of You That Are Searching

The Bible promises that when you sincerely ask God for forgiveness and trust in Jesus, you will experience new life in Christ.

That if you confess with your mouth, "Jesus is Lord," and believe in your heart that God raised him from the dead, you will be saved. — Romans 10:9

Today, with all your heart, surrender your life to Jesus Christ. Confess your sins. Ask God to forgive you. Say that you'll trust in Jesus. And thank Him for the gift of everlasting life. Pray now:

"Father, I know that I have sinned against You. Please forgive me. Wash me clean. I promise to trust in Jesus, Your Son. I believe that He died for me — He took my sin upon Himself when He died on the cross. I believe that He was raised from the dead. I surrender my life to Jesus today.

"Thank You, Father, for Your gift of forgiveness and eternal life. Please help me to live for you. In Jesus' name, Amen."

There is nothing magical about the words you use. It is the attitude of your heart that God cares about.

Acknowledgements

Thank you, Jesus! This story had been slow cooking in my brain for about 10 years. I had completed the outline early in 2011. The bones of the story were pretty much in place. The rest of the story came together very quickly. It seemed to pour out, like someone opened a hydrant for a drink of water. I sat down on December 23, 2012 to begin to put meat on the bones and at 11:45 on December 31, 2012, the story was complete. Then it got really hard. It is virtually impossible to self-edit a novel, so I relied heavily on friends and a professional editor. I would like to thank everyone who so very generously helped me complete this project.

Thank you Karin, Danielle and David for your love and support.

Julian Gonzalez – Thank you for the idea for the scene at the mall. It was a lot of fun to write, and it turned out to be one of my favorite scenes in the book.

Very special thanks to Fr. David McBriar, O.F.M. Thank you for all of your wonderful observations and your inspiration. I struggled with the very last page. Fortunately, I found the inspiration I needed in your Easter homily, from your book, *Forget Something – Homilies for Travelers.* Thanks for your dedication and service in bringing the message of Jesus to the people of so many parishes and also for being an advocate for social justice in our world.

To all my friends and colleagues at The Catholic Community of St. Francis of Assisi thank you for sharing your faith and for your friendship and support. A special thanks to Pat Kowite, Tricia Downs, and Sue Mathys for beta reading and proofing the book.

Dalinda and Bruce – Thanks for the gift of a large rabbit ornament. I had absolutely no idea what I would do with it.

Thank you to my parents for their love and sacrifice.

Diogenes Ruiz

About the Author

I enjoy writing stories that deal with the struggles between good and evil and that highlight the implications of the choices we make. I didn't start out to be a writer and perhaps after reading this book some of you are thinking, "Yup, that's the last thing you'll ever be, Chico!" It's my daughter's fault. She got me hooked on Dean Koontz and Stephen King novels. Then, one day, the writing bug cornered me and zapped me into submission. I hope that the vast majority of you will want to read my next novel, *Persistent Evil*. It picks up where *A Rabbit's Tale, An Easter Story* ends.

Persistent Evil:

What if you discovered that your life was not really your life, and your free will not really your own? Fr. Oliver confronts a bizarre and frightening truth as he helps a stranger figure out who he really is. But Fr. Oliver has troubles of his own. He keeps getting kicked out of the parishes where he serves. He is saving souls, but he cannot reveal what he sees, or else people will die. How is he supposed to serve God? Discover the terrifying reality that Fr. Oliver must confront.

Persistent Evil, look for it on Amazon.com.

To My Readers

Thank you for reading *A Rabbit's Tale An Easter Story*. Whether you share my faith or not, I hope that you enjoyed it, and I hope that you got something out of it. To those among you who do not have a relationship with Jesus Christ, I hope that reading this book helps you keep your mind and heart open to the possibility of the wonderful gift of faith.

I encourage you to write and let me know your thoughts.

Email: diogenesruiz@live.com

Facebook: https://www.facebook.com/DiogenesRuizAuthor

Website: http://www.diogenesruiz.com

Made in the USA
Charleston, SC
14 November 2014